D0188215

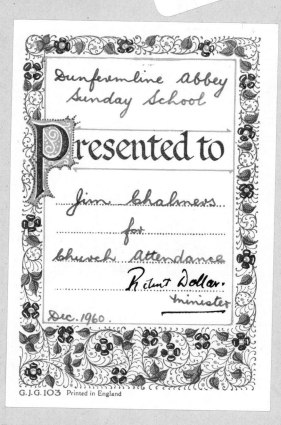

Dunfermline Abbey
Sunday School

Presented to

Jim Chalmers

for

Church Attendance

Robert Dollar.
Minister

Dec. 1960.

G.J.G. 103 Printed in England

A SPY AT MONKS' COURT

A Spy At Monks' Court

TREVOR BURGESS

HUTCHINSON OF LONDON

HUTCHINSON & CO. (*Publishers*) LTD
178–202 Great Portland Street, London, W.1

London Melbourne Sydney
Auckland Bombay Toronto
Johannesburg New York

This edition 1960

*This book has been set in Baskerville type
face. It has been printed in Great Britain by
Taylor Garnett Evans & Co. Ltd., Watford,
Herts, and bound by them*

CONTENTS

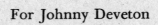

For Johnny Deveton

I

THE KID FROM SOUTH AMERICA

'THE old place hasn't changed a bit!' said Bob
Mayfield, dropping a pile of books with a prodigious
report onto the floor. The Study trembled.

'Same old view from the window. . . .' grunted
Gregory Stevens.

'Same tables, same chairs,' nodded Jim Raymond,
looking round the room after his three weeks'
absence.

'In fact,' declared Dresley Burgess, as he heard
a familiar sound from the passage outside, 'there's
only one thing missing, and that's—' He was
interrupted by a knock on the door.

'Hello, you men!' smirked a large round visage,
inserting its shining shape round the open door.

'—And that is no longer missing!' grinned Burgess,
slinging an apple in the direction of the newcomer.

'All present and correct!' sang out the irrepressible
Bob Mayfield, as the visitor shot out a fat hand and
caught the apple neatly. 'How are you, Falstaff? Fit
for a nice long Summer Term?'

Horatio Pomeroy Pepys applied his considerable

molars to the apple, ravished it at a blow, and ruminated with an expression of much appreciation. At the beginning of term the fellows of Study Four were ever wont to exhibit greater generosity than at other times; and although it would be uncharitable to suggest that for this very reason had the rotund Pepys paid this social call on the first day back in School, it was nevertheless a definite coincidence. He munched his fruit complacently for a moment while his eyes roved the scene before him.

'Thank you, Burgess,' he munched cheerfully. 'I must say you were always a chap for sharing anything you have.'

'Which means, I suppose,' grinned Greg Stevens, 'that he differs from little us?' And a ripe blood-orange sang across the room, catching the portly visitor on his starboard ear before he stayed its peregrinations with a well-aimed grab.

'Any more contributions for our worthy cause?' chuckled Jim Raymond.

'Many more, my sons!' cried the beefy Mayfield, boxing champion of Winston House. 'Here's my old soccer boots – catch!'

Pepys ducked as the boot banged against the lintel of the door, then dived as it descended, missing his parting by a hair's-width.

'Ass!' he hooted, retreating a little.

'Would you like a pair?' asked Bob Mayfield as his hand fumbled in his locker.

'That's nice of you, old chap . . .' began Pomeroy (since a pear was a fitting companion to an apple and an orange).

'Then here it comes, Podger my friend!' – and the other boot whirled through the air, landing within inches of a fat left foot as Podger Horatio turned and flashed into the passage with his orange. The apple was already eaten, and he had little desire for the sort of 'pear' that Mayfield had alluded to. The door of the Study slammed as he gave it a push.

'How nice to see old Podger again,' chuckled Dresley, sorting out his cricket gear. 'Same old face—'

'Same old trousers,' nodded Gregory Stevens, 'well filled and shining and ready for a fives-bat if he comes raiding our tuck while we're at the nets.'

'Same old appetite,' added Jim Raymond – and then another knock came on their door.

'All ye who enter here,' sang out Bob, getting ready with another soccer boot in case, 'abandon hope and glory!'

The door opened, and the boot trembled in his hand. But this was a different visitor.

'I wonder if you could put me right for Study Six, please?'

Jim Raymond looked round from the window, through which he had been gazing, remembering other Summer Terms. Dres Burgess turned from his cricket-bag and quizzed the caller. Gregory Stevens glanced up from the books he was fitting into the corner-shelves, ready for 'prep'. Bob Mayfield dropped his boot onto the floor of his locker and nodded.

'Along the passage, first left, first left again,' he

9

said cheerfully. 'It sort of backs onto this one, side-ways, the other way round, if you get it.'

'Are you del Pino?' asked Jim Raymond with interest.

'That's it,' said the new fellow.

He was tall, and his face was tanned, considering that Summer was yet to come. His dark, level eyes took in the faces of the Study-mates at a single yet calculating glance.

'Give our love to your brother-resident in Study Six,' said Dresley, concealing a smile.

'He's just left us,' nodded Gregory, poker-faced.

The new chap noted the slight atmosphere of mild amusement during these cryptic comments, but forbore to question.

'Thanks,' he said, and closed the door quietly.

'Should have warned him,' grunted Bob Mayfield.

'About what?' asked Gregory.

'His Study-mate.'

'He'll find out about Horatio Pomeroy soon enough,' said Jim Raymond, 'without our blackening his fat character for him.'

'How did you know his name?' queried Gregory Stevens, sorting out the belongings he had brought from home.

'I was talking to old Jacko at the station. Apparently this chap's been at school in South America until now.'

'Doesn't have an accent,' declared Dres Burgess, 'and he looks English enough except for his tan.'

'What's he like with the giddy willow?' Gregory wanted to know.

'Don't believe he's ever played cricket before.'

'Oh, my sainted stumps! Then he'll have to be larned!'

'Give him a few days,' grinned Jim Raymond, 'then you can take him down to the nets, Gregory, and show him one end of the bat from the ball. We'll watch, and pass the hat round when you've finished. Exhibition fees, you know.'

'Tiffin!' said Dresley, hearing the bell.

'Roll up and roll out the Swiss-roll!' sang out Gregory; and in a moment the four of them were trooping in a body along the passage and down the main stairs into West Hall. They had not reached the tables before a large figure teetered upon its corpulent heels and rolled in their direction.

'Know what, you fellows?'

'We do,' said Bob, striding onwards to the scenes of victualling. 'The Russians are in Moscow!'

'Queen Anne has passed away,' said Dresley. 'Most regrettable. . . .'

'Drake he was a Devon man,' said Greg Stevens.

'You see, Friar Tuck,' grinned Jim Raymond as they sat down, 'there's nothing you can tell us that we don't already know.'

'I'm sure I don't wish to bore you with information,' said Podger Pepys with a shrug. But he sat down alongside the Company of Four and proceeded to bore them with his information.

'I'm sure it's nothing of much note,' he continued, prising a large portion of toast from the rack, 'but I might just mention in passing—'

11

'Talking of passing,' cut in Bob cheerfully, 'you're a bit nearer the jam than I – would you mind . . . ?'

'As usual,' murmured Dresley.

'I might just mention,' went on the imperturbable Podge, 'that I've just been discussing the situation in Java with my friend the Ambassador's son.'

And he shook his head wisely, helping himself to a liberal complement of strawberry jam before relinquishing it into the hands of Mayfield.

'Java?' inquired Jim Raymond. 'Is there a war on there?'

'I mean the Yukon,' corrected Podger. 'A delicate situation, I can assure you.'

'Ambassador's son?' asked Dresley.

'The Vice-Consul's nephew, that is,' nodded the rotund romancer. 'He happens to be my Study-mate, you know. Most interesting chap.'

'Oh, really?' queried Greg Stevens in the most innocent tones. 'Is he very well-off, d'you happen to know?'

'Well-*off*?' grinned Pepys. 'My dear chap, he's a millionaire! He's brought a hamper of tuck with him as big as – I mean – I mean, how should I know? Hardly a decent question, I must say!'

'Poor old del Pino,' murmured Dresley.

'Very sad,' nodded Greg Stevens. 'Begins his term a millionaire—'

'—And ends it as a pauper,' grinned Bob Mayfield. 'By which time our personal steamroller will have burst his boilers on South American tuck!'

'Really, Mayfield,' frowned Pepys indignantly.

'Yes, really and truly,' nodded Bob.

'I might tell you . . .' began their eager informant again.

'Thank goodness it isn't a certainty!' said Dresley, relieving his fat neighbour of the butterdish for a moment.

'Of course, we can't all invite the confidence of such distinguished people as diplomats' nephews,' persisted Pepys importantly.

'We certainly can't,' nodded Bob, 'it's hard work, after all.'

'It assuredly is, Mayfield – I mean of course it isn't. They take one look at you, and decide there and then if you're likely to make an intelligent friend or not.'

'It's time you actually showed yourself to your Study-mate, Podge,' murmured Greg Stevens.

'Showed myself? Of course I have! I—'

'But you said he's a friend of yours?'

'And he's actually seen you!' grinned Jim Raymond. 'Can't have it both ways, old chap.'

'I'm sure I don't comprehend your meaning, Raymond.'

'But my intelligent friends do,' said Jim, and nudged the discomfited gossip in his well-upholstered ribs. 'Is that your own personal dish of cakes, old bean, or are you only hiring it for the evening?'

'I can see it's of no interest to you fellows,' retorted Podger Pepys, 'that we have among us a distinguished visitor from a distant country—'

'It's of very great interest, Podgy,' cut in Dresley, and turned to Jim Raymond. 'Remember that Chinese envoy's kid who was here a couple of years ago?'

'What, the chap that knifed his Study-mate with a twelve-inch stiletto?' asked Jim innocently.

'That's the bird – Hoo Fling Tong!'

'Not the one who tortured his room-mate with the fire-tongs?' gasped Mayfield.

'Yes – and remember the Hungarian Rotarian who poisoned his Study-mate's porridge with aspic and tartar? Queer types, these foreigners.'

Jim Raymond laid a comforting hand on Podger Pepys's trembling arm.

'Don't worry, Podge – the first time you see del Pino pull a knife, come along to our Study and we'll rally round!'

'If it isn't too late,' said Bob sadly, munching a shortcake with much shaking of his head.

'I s-say,' piped up the hapless Podge, 'you d-don't think . . .'

'These days,' sighed Gregory, 'you just don't know what to think.'

'All you can do is to arm yourself against all danger,' Dresley affirmed seriously.

'Oh m-my s-suffering—'

'Never mind, Podgy, he may be harmless.'

'Mind you, they often keep pet cobras in their tuck-boxes, these South American chaps.'

'Not dangerous, unless they're provoked, of course.'

'But tricky – definitely tricky.'

'Oh c-cripes! Oh m-my sainted j-jim-jams!' murmured Pepys the purveyor of important portents, swallowing a bun as though it were of sawdust. And in a moment he was seen to waddle off dismally from the tea-tables, his eyes darting nervously around him.

'Well,' chuckled Jim Raymond, the leader of the Company of Four, 'if Podger moves out of Study Six tomorrow, that man del Pino can't say we haven't done him a good turn!'

Their unkind discussion of the habits of foreigners at Monks' Court was over, but the butt of their youthful humour had fled. But it was the same night when Jim Raymond and his friends came up against del Pino unexpectedly for the second time that day – and in the most curious circumstances.

2

CLASH OF WILLS

'BLAIRMAN!'
  'Here.'
  'Burns!'
  'Present, Chief.'
  'Cass Minor!'
  'Adsum.'
  'Del Pino!'
Jim Raymond stopped, and looked round.
'Del Pino!' he repeated.
'Not here, apparently,' said Bob Mayfield.
'See if you can find him, Bob. Evans!'
  'Here.'
  'Fielding!'
  'Here.'
And by the time Jim Raymond was down to the
Y's, his friend with the beefy physique was approach-
ing the door of Study Six, in case the new fellow had
dozed off over a book during the evening.
  Bob tapped lightly on the door.
  'Who is there?'
Now, ordinarily, such a question could be inter-

preted as meaning 'come in' among the Studies of Winston House. It was the unwritten and unspoken law that no fellow should go barging into another's Study without knocking; but, having knocked, and having received a reply, he was at liberty to sail in, having thus warned the inmate of his arrival.

Bob sailed in – or he tried to. With a quick turn of the handle and a light push, he began walking forward – and stopped suddenly. Even the mighty Mayfield was unable to walk through solid panels. He rubbed his nose reflectively.

'Is that you, del Pino?'

'One moment!'

For a moment there was silence; then the key sounded in the lock, the handle was turned, and the door was opened.

'Well?'

Bob regarded the South American steadily.

'This may sound awfully silly, old bean, but we have such a thing as a roll-call before dormer. I came to ask you along.'

'You – you mean we have to leave our Studies by a certain hour?'

'It's one of our quaint old customs,' nodded Bob. He was not usually disposed to dispense sarcasm, especially to a new man; but at the moment his nose was aching from its recent contact with the door. 'Better come up with me; I'll show you the way.'

He turned aside as he spoke, confident that his offer would be accepted.

'I am afraid I am studying.'

Bob halted, and glanced back incredulously. There

were one or two industrious chaps in Winston whose ambition was centred in the end-of-term examinations and their results; but there were none who were such hogs for work that they elected voluntarily to remain in their rooms after dormer roll-call in order to extend their learning. Here, obviously, was one exception.

Bob put on a cheerful expression, to control his own slight annoyance.

'I hate to bore you, del Pino, but in the ordinary way to be missing from roll-call is to invite a rap on the knuckles. In this case you're new, though you should have got the rules into your head by now. So Head Boy sent me to find you. Coming?'

'Please tell him I shall be up presently, and that I shall give no cause for trouble. I am merely studying. Thank you for coming, however, I appreciate that.'

And before Bob Mayfield had really recovered from his amazement, he was staring at the panels of a closed door.

'Well, well, well . . .' he murmured, and shrugged, going back along the corridor and climbing the staircase above West Hall to Long Dormer.

'Got a message for you, Jim,' he told his chief as he strolled among the beds.

Jim Raymond looked up as he folded his trousers over a hanger.

'Did you find del Pino?' he asked.

'I did. He asked me to give you a diplomatic note. He says sorry, and all that, but he's studying.'

'He's *what*?'

'What for,' grinned Dresley Burgess from the next bed, 'his B.A.?'

Bob gave Raymond a rough outline of what had happened at the door of Study Six, and finished with a shrug. 'If you still want him, Jim, you'd better go and bring him up by his ear. I'm turning in.'

A moment later the leader of the famous Quartet was tapping at the door of Study Six. Bob had told him about his nose and the effect of sudden wood upon it, so Jim did not make the same mistake. After del Pino had opened the door, Raymond said:

'Sorry, but you'll have to stop work. Bed-time.'

'It is not yet ten-thirty.'

'Roll-call is at ten-fifteen, del Pino. You missed that, and could be reported. Obviously you've an excuse, being new here; but now I'm asking you to come up to dormer. Well?'

'I appreciate your concern,' said del Pino easily, 'but I am studying. Surely that makes an exception to the rule.'

'Are you coming freely,' said Jim steadily, 'or do I take you up by force? Quick!'

Already nettled by the cool message Bob had passed on to him, he was in no mood to put up with further clowning. The new chap was taller than Jim Raymond by a couple of inches, and his frame was athletic and muscular; but the head of the Fourth could back his authority with a good straight left if the occasion arose.

'What if I refuse?' asked del Pino, blocking the doorway and gazing calmly enough at Raymond.

'Ordinarily I'd merely trot along to Mr. Jackersby's

room, and ask him to take what action he thought fit,' said Jim evenly. 'But as I don't much care for reporting chaps to the beaks, especially on their first day in Winston, I shall prefer to exert my own authority and – pull you all the way to the dormer by your ear. Is that quite understood?'

For a moment del Pino hesitated, perhaps wondering just how far he could go in his obstinacy. Then he smiled; and there was something quite friendly about this fellow's grin when he chose to show it.

'I should say we are about evenly matched, Raymond. It would therefore be an interesting tug-of-war. But I appreciate that your position as Head Boy makes it difficult for you, having to give orders to your own Form-mates. I shall not aggravate your difficulties.'

With which gracious speech he turned into the Study, put his book on the shelf, and came back, closing the door quietly. Jim said nothing on their way up to Long Dormer. He was a little angered by the smooth tongue of the South American; and there had been the subtle implication that it might have been more than the Head Boy could do to take del Pino by his ear to bed. Jim almost wished the new fellow had persisted a little longer in his obstinacy, so that he could have had the excuse of backing his words.

'Well, well . . .' murmured Gregory Stevens, as Raymond came in with del Pino. 'Our Bachelor of Arts has finally come to roost!'

'Didn't take Jim very long to make the kid see sense,' grunted Dres Burgess.

Their chief stood over del Pino as the new man tugged his shoes off and placed them on the rack.

'Just one other thing,' he said quietly. 'There are keys to most of the doors of the Studies, but we don't like their being used. D'you mind?' And he held his hand out.

Del Pino eyed him in genuine surprise.

'But I have property there, valuable property.'

'Then let Mr. Jackersby have it. He'll see that it's stored for you in the safe and you'll be given a receipt.'

'I – I mean there are books, and other things that I use every day. They are irreplaceable in this country.'

'Taking it by and large,' said Raymond succinctly, 'we don't have many thieves in Winston. The key, please.'

'Why did you let me lock the door when you were down there with me, if it's not allowed?'

'Because I had an idea you'd argue about it, and I didn't want a beak to come along and find us out of the dormer, because I should have had to give an explanation, and that would have been awkward for you.'

'You – knew I would argue?' – and there was the ghost of a smile curving the fellow's firm, straight mouth.

'Yes,' Jim nodded briefly. 'You're the type, I can see that easily enough.'

'Is it in the rules of the School – about locking the Study doors?'

'In the unwritten rules, yes. Your Study-mate, Pepys, has as much right as you to lock the door – and there aren't two keys. One of you hasn't the right to lock the other out at any time of the day. I'm not going to say any more, now that I've explained the position to you. The key, please.'

As before, del Pino hesitated, as though wondering how far he could go before the Head Boy became really serious. As he hesitated, he and Raymond were aware that a hush had come to the dormer, and ten or twelve fellows were lying on their beds with their heads turned in his direction. There was come a clash of wills; and the outcome was going to prove interesting.

Do you always make things difficult when you find yourself in new surroundings, del Pino?'

'No, but sometimes things are made difficult for me.'

That was checkmate.

'You're hardly going the right way about easing the situation, then.'

'If I hand you the key, Raymond, you will have to be responsible for the safety of my property.'

'I shall certainly not, del Pino. Nor shall I be responsible for my own actions, if you don't do as I ask very quickly.'

He turned away, but del Pino stopped him.

'Here you are, Raymond.'

The key was held out in the palm of his hand.

Jim took it, nodding.

'Good. You can have it back in the morning, and you'll put it back in the door right away. After which you won't take it out again, locked or unlocked. That clear?'

'Quite clear, thank you.'

'I'm glad you can see sense, even though it takes you some time. Good night, del Pino.'

'Good night, Raymond.'

As Jim made for his own bed-space, a snigger of amusement broke the tension that had reigned in the room since the clash of wills had first begun.

'Trust Raymond to tell a new kid where he gets off!'

Jim paused, and shot an angry glance in the direction of the sniggerer.

'Get into bed, Pepys, and can it!' he snapped sharply.

Podger Horatio Pomeroy Pepys had the sudden grace to desist from his comments. The springs of his bed twanged like half a dozen guitars as they received his weight, and their complaint was loud and unmelodious.

'Difficult type,' murmured Dresley Burgess, as Jim slipped his dressing-gown on and slung a towel over his shoulder.

'I don't know what sort of school he was at in South America,' replied Raymond reflectively, 'but there wasn't much discipline there. It's not entirely his fault,' and he pottered off to the bath-rooms, turning out the lights as he went through the doorway. In ten minutes he was back, to find his own particular friends half asleep. The dormer was quiet, except for the sounds of steady breathing.

Turning in, Jim Raymond stared for a few moments at the faint glow of the starlight on the ceiling, thinking over the events of the last half-hour. Much as he regretted his having to show the fist to a new kid on his first day in Winston, he couldn't have justified any other alternative.

Sleep came at last to the leader of the Company of Four; but in the bed a few yards distant from his own del Pino remained wakeful a few minutes longer; and he was also going over the events of the last half-hour.

A third fellow in Long Dormer was still sleepless, and his corpulent form was visible above his bed, like – as Bob Mayfield had once put it – 'a drum on a pea'. Podger Pepys was thinking deeply, and it was natural that the unaccustomed effort of such a harrowing procedure should keep him awake for some minutes after most of the other chaps had dozed to their dreams. Podger Pepys was thinking of what that new kid had told Raymond – about there being 'valuable property' in Study Six.

Pepys was piqued. His inquisitive intellect savoured the possibilities. Valuable? Property? In what form? Gold bullion, smuggled from South America and on its way to some European bank? Priceless gems, brought to England to save them from dark-skinned robbers in the steaming jungles (or was it freezing wastes of ice and snow? Pepys's geography was somewhat sketchy) of the Latin Continent?

Remembering the conversation of tea-time, he gave a shiver. A pet cobra might be called 'valuable property' – the London Zoo paid enormous prices for specimens.

The portly Podge composed himself at last for slumber; but his last waking thought was that he must lose no time in making personal and confidential inquiries into the contents of his own Study. Chaps couldn't go about littering the place with gold bullion, diamonds and cobras.

Chaps couldn't – go about – cluttering the place – with golden bulls and – diamond cobras. Chaps couldn't – go bullion about – cobbling wobbling diadems – and . . .

And sleep came to the confused thoughts of H. Pomeroy Pepys. Sleep, and dreams of Study Six, knee-deep in priceless booty from far-flung El Dorado.

3

CALAMITY IN THE WIND

FOR a while it seemed as though the new kid, del Pino, was prepared to settle down and, being in Winston, to do as the Winstonians did. The affair of the Study-door key and the absence from roll-call was forgotten, except perhaps by Podger H. P. Pepys, whose memory was as capacious as it was undiscriminating. Horatio Pomeroy was wont to forget entirely all those things he ought not to forget (such as Pythagoras, Byron and the chief export of Tanganyika), and to remember all those things that were (*a*) trivial and unimportant, (*b*) by far best forgotten and (*c*) untrue in the first place. He therefore remembered the little scene between Jim Raymond and del Pino; and remembered the mention of 'valuable property'; and thought much upon the implications of such an admission by the newcomer to Monks' Court.

True, Gregory Stevens was doing his best to provide some kind of variety to the proceedings. Greg was, in many ways, a seeker after the unusual. He was not a boy, for example, to devote very much attention to birds'-nesting, stamp-collecting or model railways. This had been done before, and would be done again, down the ages of adolescence. For Gregory there must needs be some less ordinary pursuit, something more original.

So he had designed a kite.

It is true enough that a kite is no more unusual a matter for the attention of a schoolboy than is a thrush's egg, a Burmese overprint (obsolete) or a Hornby loco. But with Gregory Stevens's kite there was a difference. He had thought of the design during the holidays, and the kite was almost completed by the time Term started. He had brought it with him, and within three days of his return to the ancient seat of learning he had finished the work. It was on the first Sunday after the beginning of Term that he took his three friends down to South Meadow, the great sweep of grassland just across the Radford road, in order to demonstrate the unusual capabilities of his kite.

Bob Mayfield was frankly sceptical.

'No kite,' he said firmly, 'with that many gadgets and levers and spindles and strings,' he went on, 'can possibly carry its own weight,' he added soberly, 'into the air.'

'Not even in a gale,' agreed Dresley Burgess.

Gregory said nothing. They were standing in a group at the wider end of the Meadow, down which a slow south wind was moving, between Monks' Court and Banner Wood.

'But seeing's believing,' said Jim Raymond; and they waited to see and, if possible, to believe.

'I ought to show you chaps the extreme cleverness of the design,' Gregory told them modestly, 'before I give a demonstration. She's got three strings, for one thing.'

'The more strings to one's kite the better,' murmured Dresley, 'or is it "bow"?'

'The middle string, which is tougher than the others,' went on Stevens, ignoring the facetious Burgess, 'serves the purpose as with ordinary kites.'

'It joins the thing to the ground,' nodded Bob Mayfield. 'Jolly clever, that.'

'The other two strings,' said Gregory, frowning darkly into the broad and innocent countenance of the simple sportsman, 'are operated by these two levers, and connect them to a pair of swivelling flaps on the canvas of the kite.'

'Snivelling taps,' murmured Dresley, nodding at this wisdom; 'very scientific, that is, I'd say.'

'When I pull the left one,' said Gregory, turning his back on Burgess, 'the left flap closes and the right one opens, and the kite starts to swerve to the left.'

'How d'you know which is the right one?' asked Jim Raymond gently.

'There can only be one right one, Jim,' explained the mischievous Mayfield on Greg's behalf, 'because the other one is the one that's left. I mean, it's perfectly simple. Go on, Greg, I can't stand the suspense.'

Gregory forbore to proceed with his gratuitous lecture. The opposition was too great. There was only one way to show these fellows whether or not he could design, build and fly a super-kite – and that was to fly it.

So, making no reference to the other levers, vanes, flaps, ribs and pulley-wheels, Gregory took his enormous ratchet-winder in one hand, and held the kite – which stood a good five feet from the ground – upwards to the wind.

Now, in the ordinary way, a chap has to run pretty nimbly with a kite that size to get it airborne. Not so with the Stevens Special. Moving a small lever of balsa-wood near the tail of the kite, he tilted two horizontal flaps near the top: and it happened, as simply as that. As though pulled upwards by an invisible string, the kite lifted to the wind, while the ratchet of the winder clicked merrily in Gregory's hand. In a moment it was a dozen feet up; in two minutes it was sailing serenely, fifty feet above the heads of the astonished audience, with no sound, no fuss, no trouble.

The broad features of the boxing champion of Winston wore an expression of stupefaction as he gazed upwards. Dresley Burgess goggled. Jim Raymond blinked in amazement. Above them sailed the extraordinary-looking device, rising with every minute as the winder ran out on its smoothly working ratchet.

'G-great giggling gollywogs!' gasped Mayfield.

'Greg, you're a giddy genius!' declared Burgess.

'First time I've ever seen a kite go straight upwards from a standing start!' confessed Jim Raymond.

Secretly delighted with this first success – for he was not to know that the new kite would perform in practice what theory claimed – Gregory controlled his excitement.

'Not very satisfactory,' he said casually, and even managed a slight tone of disappointment in his words. 'But then, of course, there's hardly any wind, considering the size of the kite.'

'Show us more!' demanded Bob Mayfield, unashamed of his former scepticism.

'What d'you want it to do?' asked Gregory in an off-hand tone.

'Make it loop the loop!' Jim Raymond suggested.

Gregory nodded. The kite was some hundred feet above them, hovering over the centre of the Meadow. At the moment it was perfectly motionless, for he had put the lock on the ratchet-winder. Now, with an easy movement of the little lever on the left of the winding-frame, he jerked the left-hand string. It quivered, tautening, and the ripple of its movement ran upwards along its length until, a moment later, it reached the flap which it controlled, and opened it. At once the kite swerved to the left, dipping gracefully down . . . down . . . until it curved under and began rising to the right, in a perfectly controlled loop.

'Full – *marks*!' breathed Jim Raymond, his head tilted backwards as he gazed above him.

'We'll make it a figure-of-eight,' grunted Stevens, and he flicked the right-hand lever in the same moment. As the kite reached the apex of its loop, the right-hand flap opened, and it rose, curving round and then swerving downwards in a second and higher loop, finishing up motionless in its former position, hovering as steadily as a cloud over the centre of South Meadow.

'You're wasting your time, Greg' – Dresley shook his head – 'learning Latin.'

'It wants adjusting, of course,' replied the expert, grinning in spite of himself. 'But I admit it wasn't a bad show.' He released the winder and the kite rose another twenty feet or so; and then, just as he was thinking up a new manœuvre to demonstrate its further powers, Bob Mayfield said:

'Hello, hello! What do I glimpse before my eyes but the familiar figure of our own personal Steam-roller, plying in our direction!'

They followed his gaze, and saw the unmistakable form of Podger Pepys, walking briskly across the Radford road, his large face lifting now and then to gape at the kite above the field.

'P. H. Pomeroy P., in person!' chuckled Dresley; 'come, doubtless, to allow full rein to his overwhelming curiosity upon this eventful Sabbath.'

Gregory gave a sudden grin.

'Now I can really show you a trick or two!' he said, and his hand flicked one of the control-levers on the winder.

As Bob, Jim and Dresley watched, puzzled but expectant, Gregory brought the kite swooping down to the left. Even from the ground they could hear the whining of the wind through the flaps and past the struts as it slipped sideways against the clear blue sky, heading as a great and enraged hornet – for that plump and rolling figure.

'Look out, Greg!' gasped Jim Raymond – then he

swallowed hard in relief as Gregory, timing his programme to a nicety, snapped down the right-hand lever. The kite shivered once as the flap-control operated; then with a whine of the air-stream it swerved viciously, droning above Pepys's head with less than twelve inches to spare. Even from this distance his hoot of terror was deafeningly audible:

'*Whoops!* Keep off! Take it away!' – and he picked himself up from the grass, where he had thrown himself flat – or as flat as anything barrel-shaped can throw itself – and came running towards the group of fellows, red with indignation.

'Poor old Podge!' roared Bob Mayfield, with tears of merriment starting from his eyes.

'*Yawps!*' hooted Pepys, sprinting like a mobile whale. 'Keep it off, you bounders! *He-elp*, it's after me!'

Gregory showed mercy at last. As the terrified fat-man rolled up to them, palpitating in every ponderous portion of his portly personage, the kite sheered off, to hang motionless over the middle of the field, as though pretending innocence of any mischief.

'Sorry, Podger,' grinned the unrepentant Gregory; 'it got out of control.'

'Then you should know better,' spluttered Pepys indignantly, 'than to allow such a dangerous device to get out of hand! It nearly got me!'

'I thought it did,' nodded Bob Mayfield; 'in fact we were afraid it was going to be smashed to pieces on your head.'

'What about my head?' hooted the outraged Pomeroy.

'Oh, I doubt if anything could make a dent in that, old bean,' chuckled Dres Burgess.

Podger Pepys sat himself down on the grass to regain his breath and to watch – with the wariest possible eye – the extraordinary device that was now flying higher and higher above the Radford road.

'How much higher can it go?' gasped Dresley, straining his eyes against the sunlit sky.

'There's half a mile of twine,' Gregory said briefly.

In silence they watched the kite diminishing in size and detail as the winder's ratchet span slowly, paying out the twine.

'It must be over the School grounds by now!' Jim Raymond said at last.

'It is – and that's as far as we can go until we get some more twine. Tomorrow I'm going down to the village to—' But Greg Stevens broke off. He had felt an uneasy movement along the string, vibrating the winder. A moment later the kite dipped, and went into a straining swerve to the left.

'What's up?'

'Look out – she's dropping!'

Greg tugged, snapping the twin levers desperately.

'Struck an air-current over the buildings,' he said, jerking the string steadily and releasing. But the kite was out of control in real earnest this time. Twice it slewed, swinging drunkenly towards a wall of the great pile of masonry that was Monks' Court; and twice he brought it out by jerking the right-hand lever to counteract the drift. But the third time, calamity came. As he pulled the lever there was a snap, and the taut string went slack.

'Flap out of action!' he panted desperately.

A moment later – for sound travels relatively slowly – they heard the unmistakable crash of flying glass.

There came silence.

Bob Mayfield put his large hands into his pockets and pursed his lips in a whistle.

'Oh well,' murmured Dresley, 'it's been a very pleasant day – up to now.'

'Come on, you chaps,' Jim Raymond sighed, 'let's get it over.'

Together the Company of Four, with their companion whose curiosity had nearly led to his being crowned on the cranium, moved slowly across South Meadow towards the Radford road and, beyond it, the mellow pile of masonry whose hundreds of windows were now decreased . . . by one.

4

SHARP ENCOUNTER

THERE was a buzz of comment as fifty or sixty fellows, some from Winston, some from Charlton, stood in a crowd at the corner of the West Hall, gazing up at the kite – or the remains of it – that had just written off a complete window. Among them now were Jim Raymond, Dres Burgess, Bob Mayfield, and Gregory Stevens; not to mention Podger Horatio P. Pepys himself.

'Well,' murmured Jim, 'one of us had better cut along and climb the turret from the inside.'

'I'll have a try,' nodded Gregory, but as he made to go into the building Jim put a hand on his arm.

'I shouldn't, old bean,' he said gently. 'Any minute now and there'll be a beak on the scene – and the name of the culprit will be wanted. I hate to remind you, but he's you. So we can't tell the beak you're inside a turret – and out of bounds. That's what they call adding insult to injury. I'll try to get the kite down while you're – chatting with the authorities.'

'Right-o,' grinned Gregory sheepishly. 'I'll wait here like the lamb for the slaughter, don't worry.'

'If I thought there was any chance of getting away with it scot free,' Jim murmured, 'we'd have a try. But several chaps have seen us with the kite-string, and old Podge would be bound to tell, unintentionally or on purpose. Might as well take our medicine while it's fresh.'

Saying which, he moved out of the fringe of the crowd and made his way into the West doors, climbing the first flight of stairs past the Hall to the corridors where were the Studies. His prophecy was accurate, for a few minutes after he had gone a tall figure was seen approaching from the East wing of Winston House.

The buzz of comment broke up.

'Psst! Beak!'

'Scatter, you men!'

'Here comes Nemesis!'

'Well, I'm going . . .'

And before Mr. Jackersby, Housemaster of Winston, had reached the spot immediately below the dangling ruins of the kite he found no more than a handful of fellows. These, however, included three of the Company of Four.

Mr. Jackersby stopped, tilted his head to peer upwards at the cause of the breaking glass, looked down again, and said:

'Who flew that kite up there?'

'It was me, sir,' spoke up Gregory.

Mr. Jackersby regarded him.

'On the contrary, Stevens,' he said calmly, 'it was "I".'

'*You*, sir?' gasped Gregory in amazement.

'You misunderstand me,' said Mr. Jackersby drily. 'It was not I, but, had it been, I should have admitted it by saying "it was I", and not "it was me". That clear? Question of nominative and accusative, your antecedent being "it". However, the Headmaster has asked that I should bring into his presence the boy or boys who thought fit to pass their Sabbath leisure in shattering windows. Well?'

'I'm ready, sir.'

'Only you, Stevens? Did not your friends here participate in this escapade?'

'No, sir. They – just watched. I asked them to.'

'We'll roll up, sir,' grinned Dres Burgess cheerfully, 'if you think it'd make a better show!'

Mr. Jackersby pursed his lips. It would not do to return that cheeky grin, though his mouth was more than ready to twitch with amusement.

'I require the culprit or culprits,' he said firmly. 'If no one other than Stevens is involved, then he shall come with me alone.'

For a moment he looked round.

'Where is Raymond?'

'He's – gone down to the Gym, sir,' said Bob Mayfield.

'He's gone for a walk, sir,' said Dres Burgess at the same time.

'He's – in the San, sir,' averred Gregory simultaneously, 'with – with a headache.'

Mr. Jackersby observed the trio.

'Young Raymond,' he said, 'would appear to be a man of many parts. One in the Gymnasium, one out walking, and one in the Sanatorium. Stevens, come

37

with me. You others return to the Junior Common Room, where I shall be able to find you if I require you.'

As he turned along the edge of the Quadrangle he glanced up for another glimpse of the curious kite that was the cause of the trouble. Gregory raised his eyes at the same time.

'What . . .' began Mr. Jackersby, halting in surprise.

'That's funny, sir!' suggested Gregory, for the want of a brighter comment. The kite had vanished.

'Very funny indeed,' agreed the master. Turning round, he fixed Mayfield and Burgess with a keen eye. 'I would hazard the guess that Raymond is far from being in the Gymnasium, the Sanatorium, or out walking. *I* should say he was up there.' And he pointed a finger above him without removing his gaze from the too-innocent faces of the two fellows. 'Please wait until he has returned within bounds, and ask him to step along to Dr. Ransome's Study. That's a most extraordinary-looking kite of yours, my dear Stevens,' Mr. Jackersby went on with certain interest.

'It's my own design, sir.'

'Ah. I – I so happen to have – er – watched its performance for some considerable time, before the – er – somewhat cataclysmic climax to the demonstration.'

'Really, sir?' asked Gregory, pleased that the beak was showing an intelligent interest in his design.

'Indeed yes, Stevens.' Mr. Jackersby gave a sudden chuckle as they turned a corner and entered the cool shadow of an archway. 'I've never seen young Pepys running so fast in all my days – we ought to put him into serious training for the hundred yards.'

Before they stopped outside the awesome panels, the beak said softly:

'I'd rather like to look at that design of yours, when you've got the time to spare. Rather interesting.'

Before Gregory could reply, Mr. Jackersby's knuckles had carried out a brisk tattoo upon the panels of the door; and a familiar – but highly respected – voice sounded from within.

'Come!'

With a slight cough, Mr. Jackersby opened the door. After him, forlorn and dejected, went Gregory. The door closed.

.   .   .   .   .

The J.C.R. was almost deserted on this warm Sunday afternoon, for the place was shadowed and cool. Chaps saw enough of its dark panelling and beamed ceiling on weekdays, between periods and meal-times. But Bob and Dresley were sitting on a window-seat, true to orders. It was some quarter of an hour before Gregory and Jim showed up; and when they did they were greeted with the inevitable question:

'Hello, you men – what's the verdict?'

'Did you get much of the chopper, Greg?'

Jim and Gregory came over, grinning ruefully.

'Gated for a week,' Jim said, and shrugged.

'Both of you?'

'Yes. And the cost of one window to come out of our term's tin. Oh well . . .'

'And Jacko says you can cut,' added Gregory. 'Which also goes for us.'

They strolled out into the sunshine, feeling low-spirited after the exhilarating exhibition with the super-kite and its sorry climax.

'Where's the kite, Jim?' asked Gregory, kicking a stone along the pathway between the beech-trees.

'I left it in the Study. It hasn't taken such a beating as we thought.'

'I'll have a look at it after tea. Jacko asked me if I'd show it to him some time. Decent old boy, Jacko.'

'He happens to be a bit of a designer himself, I've heard,' nodded Bob Mayfield. 'He patents model aircraft or something.'

'Take him your Window-Breaking Dreadnought this evening after Service,' said Dresley.

'I may. But I shall want some new balsa-wood and balsa-cement tomorrow, for repairs.'

'We can go down to the village for you,' nodded Bob Mayfield. 'Give us a list of the things you want.'

They turned across the Quad, making for the playing-fields. As they did so, Gregory caught sight of a pale blob in one of the windows on the South wall, and recognized it as a face; and recognized the face as that of—

'Del Pino!' he exclaimed.

His friends turned their heads.

'Where, Greg?'

'In his Study. That man just asks for trouble, doesn't he?'

For a moment they halted, looking upwards at the window of Study Six; then they walked on, down towards the First XI pitch.

'Going to warn him, Jim?' asked Dresley.

'No. He doesn't take my advice very willingly. He can find out the rest of the rules for himself.'

For it was a strict instruction at Monks' Court that on Sunday afternoons, from middle-day until tea-time, no boy was to remain in his Study. There was, of course, a good reason for this rule: enough time was spent in the Studies during the week; and on Sundays there was the chance of getting the chaps away from their more familiar haunts and encouraging them to walk in the fresh air, in the grounds, along the many country lanes in the vicinity, along the quiet towpath that edged the River Trayle, and among the fields and woody places.

'Come on,' said Bob Mayfield, 'what say we go down to the Trayle and get a boat out?'

'Seconded!' said Dresley.

'I'm in!' nodded Gregory.

'Unanimous!' said Jim Raymond; and the four of them veered across the playing-fields, making for the lower gate that would take them to the towpath by the shortest route.

From a deck-chair on the pavilion veranda, a pair of eyes watched them as they receded slowly from view across the green panorama.

Podger Horatio Pomeroy P. blinked slowly, his fat brain working over the problem that was teasing him. The Company of Four had passed within a dozen yards or so of the pavilion a few moments ago, and their remarks concerning the face in the window of Study Six had carried in the still and sunlit air.

Podger Pepys had rolled complacently down to the pavilion soon after Mr. Jackersby had dispersed the crowd below the turret window. There was no likelihood, the portly mascot of the Fourth had decided, of scrounging anything edible until teatime: the Studies were out of bounds today at this time, and in the quiet of the building a beak might hear a footstep, however stealthy; and to be discovered in the act of raiding tuck when all the owners thereof had fled, according to the rules, would be to bring upon his head the greatest possible unhappiness. It would certainly rate a whacking, to say the least.

He watched them disappearing through the lower gate, bound, apparently, for the River. So that new kid, del Pino, was in his Study, was he? *His* Study – and *Podger's* Study.

Podger blinked. He did not entirely approve of a fellow making free with his own room at any time he chose. Pepys had been a time-honoured member of Winston many months before young del Pino had appeared from half-way across the Southern Hemisphere. And Pepys, a law-abiding chap, as any would admit, had never (or seldom, anyhow) been seen in his Study on a Sunday afternoon. Yet here was the new kid, his sojourn at Monks' Court but a few days old, breaking the rules and using Study Six for his own private purposes.

It was annoying. Podger sat, annoyed.

More than that – and here, perhaps, was the real

source of his interest – it was curious. Why should del Pino want to spend so much of his time up there? After roll-call, when he should be in dormer; on Sunday afternoon, when he should be out in the grounds or beyond – why?

Podger sat, and Podger blinked, and Podger asked himself: why? Was he sitting up there scoffing tuck? So that his own Study-mate shouldn't see even a morsel? Was he training his pet cobra to play devilish tricks in the dormer or in class? Or manufacturing a cunning time-bomb with which to blow Monks' Court to bits on behalf of the South American Embassy?

The imagination (and it was considerable) of H. Pomeroy P. ran riot and, having run, came back to the immediate question. Why?

He would answer it for himself, by going and seeing.

It required but five or ten minutes' determined contemplation of his decision to force him to the unhappy conclusion that in order to go and see del Pino it would be necessary – indeed, essential – to lever himself out of his comfortable deck-chair. But this commitment, once realized, was duly made; and in less than fifteen minutes the considerable tonnage of H. Pomeroy was embarked upon its ponderous passage from the pavilion to the School buildings.

A moment later he stood outside the door of Study Six. Since it was his own Study there was, of course, no need to knock. So he merely turned the handle and pushed.

Now the panels of this particular door, like

those of all the other doors in Monks' Court, had been designed to withstand considerable pressure. So was the lock. At this moment the panels creaked under the strain, and the lock shuddered. But, as Bob Mayfield had been made to realize, a few nights before, it was not easy to pass through a doorway which contained a door that was both closed and locked.

'Oooch!' breathed the discomfited Podge, and caressed his nose, which had borne the greater part of the brunt.

'Who is there?'

Podger glared at the door, past his outraged proboscis. To be locked out of his own Study was bad enough; but to be made to suffer a personal injury upon attempting to enter it was really a fraction in excess!

'Open the door!' he commanded, more out of anger than with authority. Nevertheless, the voice of Horatio Pom., when raised in righteous wrath, was possessed of a tone comparable with that of Dr. Ransome's itself. It was, so to say, loud; not to mention unequivocal. In less than half a minute the key grated in the lock, and the door opened.

'Oh, it's you, Pepys. What do you want?'

'Look here, del Pino,' he said, employing the highest-handed tone in his considerable repertoire, 'you've simply no business to keep on bolting this door, you know! I happen to want to come into my own Study, that's all.'

And he took a pace forward, to follow up his words.

But del Pino, far from being cowed and repentant (to which humble state of mind Pepys's wrathful tones should surely have brought him), did not move. Blocking the doorway, he said calmly, and not unpleasantly:

'Sorry, Pepys, but I'm working. Would you mind very much pottering off for a while?'

'You – you refuse to let me into my own Study?' he gasped.

'I don't refuse, no. I'm just asking you.'

Still del Pino did not budge.

That did it.

'You realize, of course,' said Podge pompously, 'that you're out of bounds in there, on Sunday afternoon?'

'Then I'd advise your keeping out. You might get into trouble.'

'I think there's only one thing to be done, del Pino. I shall ask Mr. Jackersby to be good enough to step along here, right away. Perhaps he can persuade you that a new kid must learn to— *Whoops!*'

For, whatever Mr. Jackersby might persuade the new kid to do, the new kid was now persuading, with a swift jerk of his muscular hand, his Study-mate to enter his own Study: under definite compulsion. In less than a moment Podger found himself in his lawful surroundings, but in circumstances that could have been happier. For del Pino, after hauling the fat-man through the doorway, now closed the door firmly, and stood over him, pressing him with his portly back to the wall in a most menacing attitude.

'I'd advise you to forget you saw me in here this afternoon, Pepys. That clear?'

Podger gazed up into the dark, serious face.

'I – I – look here, you—'

Then he heard something click. Looking down, he saw, held firmly in that honey-brown hand, a knife. A knife with a long narrow blade and an ivory sheath, from which the blade had sprung with a metallic click.

'I want your word, Pepys. You will not mention – to anyone at all – that you found me in here when the room was out of bounds. Well?'

And the knife moved, with a tiny jerk, so that the sunbeams that slanted in through the window winked on the cold, smooth metal.

'*Well?*'

Podger Pepys trembled. From outside the building came the faint voices of fellows who were strolling about, or tossing a cricket-ball, or enjoying their Sunday afternoon in some other innocent way.

But, trapped in here with the dark-skinned South American, all Podger Pepys could hear was the echo of that wicked-looking knife; and all he could see was the sunlight, winking upon the blade.

'Oh *g-golly* . . . !' he panted miserably.

5

THE PROWLER

'RAYMOND, can I talk to you?'

'You can, little fairy!'

'Oh good.'

'Carry on, then.'

'Well, I – I mean privately.'

Jim Raymond walked on, his pace unabated. Climbing the wide flight of stairs to Long Dormer with his three boon companions, he turned his head.

'What's private with me is private with these chaps,' he said encouragingly. 'Carry on, good Podge!'

'Ope those winsome lips,' invited Bob Mayfield, taking the stairs two at a time in his usual boisterous fashion, 'and regale us with words both sweet and kindly spoke!'

'It's nothing to do with you, Mayfield, as it so happens.'

'Then I shall refuse to have anything to do with it,' said Bob firmly.

Dres and Gregory chuckled as the rotund supplicator came panting up the stairs in their wake.

'Tell all,' said Jim Raymond, reaching the corridor.

'Tell the untruth, the part-truth, and everything but the truth, as you usually do,' said Dresley.

'Raymond, I'm quite serious—'

'We've learned from bitter experience,' said Gregory, 'that it's impossible to take you lightly.'

'Kindly desist, Stevens, or I shall think about reporting you to the Head about that silly kite of yours, so there!'

'He's heard the story already – from me own honest lips, Podgy. The true story, too, which is more than he'd get from little you!'

'Really, Stevens! Raymond, I *must* talk to you privately.'

They reached the dormer, and found most of the other members of the two Fourth Forms gathered for roll-call.

'My dear Falstaff,' said Jim seriously, 'this isn't the best time for a private chat, when we're all swarming round for roll-call. See me in ten minutes or so, and then there'll be a better chance.'

Some fifteen minutes later, after the names had been called (and, miraculously, had all been answered, for it was not rare for a chap to leave School surreptitiously for some secret reason, frivolous or grave), Jim Raymond remembered Podger and his wish to commune with him. Moving over to the bed-space occupied by H. Pomeroy, Jim asked quietly:

'Well, Podgy, what was on your mind?'

'It's about that n-new kid, Raymond.'

'Del Pino?'

'Yes. He's – he's dangerous!'

'Oh?'

'Yes. He's armed to the teeth, with – with swords!'

'*Swords?*'

'I – I mean scimitars! I tell you—'

'Listen, Podge, if you've anything serious to say, I'm listening. If not—'

'I assure you, my dear Raymond, that—' and that was all Jim heard about the matter that night, for del Pino came back at that moment from the bathrooms, and made for his bed, just across the room from Podger's.

'Go on?' invited Jim Raymond, struggling to decide whether there was anything really important on the fat-man's mind or not.

'I – never s-said a thing, Raymond!'

'*What?*'

'I – d-don't know what you're t-talking about, I'm sure.'

And Podger hurried out of his oversized togs, wriggled gelatinously into his dressing-gown, and fled to the bathrooms, his towel flapping over his shoulder. Jim Raymond went back to his bed; but he had not missed the sudden change that had come over Pepys. As del Pino had entered the long room Podger had paled slightly, and had closed up like the veriest clam.

'What's up with our Dreadnought?' queried Gregory Stevens, seeing Jim Raymond's perplexed brow. 'Has he had too many dozen helpings of supper again?'

'Don't know,' Jim answered quietly. 'I'll let you know in the morning.'

In the bathrooms, Podger, as he wallowed among the steamy waters, could not forget his brief interview with the Head Boy, Jim Raymond.

It would seem that he had indeed chosen an ill time to invoke the comfort of a stronger colleague in going to Jim just before roll-call; but the fact was simply that, as soon as he had escaped the clutches of that devilish knife-thrower, the palpitating Podge had fled to the comfort of his own fat counsel; and his own counsel had advised him to obey the new kid's injunctions, and say nothing to anyone about his having been in Study Six this afternoon.

Pepys had seen Jim Raymond during tea, and again in the J.C.R. There had been more than one opportunity of confiding in him. But the memory of that long, bright blade, and the echo of those cold, calculating words, had stilled the tongue in Podger's head.

But by ten minutes past ten Podger had reached that point when he must confide in *someone* or – or bust. And so, unwilling to bust, he had at last driven his fearful footsteps in the direction of the corridor leading to the Fourth Form studies – only to find that it was too late. Jim Raymond, together with his friends from Study Four, were already on their way up to dormer; and the opportunity, so lately snatched, was lost in the same instant.

Podger mopped his face dry, tightened the cord of his dressing-gown, and returned to his bed, his mind still busily occupied with his problems.

True, the South American had done nothing more than threaten him with the knife. As soon as Pepys had sworn – which he did with alacrity – that he would never mention to anyone that del Pino had been out of bounds this afternoon, the blade had clicked back, as if by mechanical magic, into its ivory sheath; and the new kid had even given a quick smile, albeit a trifle grim.

Within a moment the part-resident of Study Six, not long ago eager to enter its familiar portals, had exited, with considerable despatch. But his problem remained, and now it was twofold. One: he was not going to enjoy being confined within the walls of his own study in the future, together with a chap who carried a weapon as wicked looking as that dagger. How to bend over his text-books of an evening, without feeling the icy blade piercing his shoulder-blades? And, two: the problem was twofold now because Podger had done that very thing which he ought not to have done. He had gone to Jim Raymond, and in another moment would have blurted out the whole story. He knew that Raymond was already aware of del Pino's presence in the Study – he had heard, from his deck-chair on the pavilion veranda, the conversation that was centred upon that very point; but del Pino would believe that Podger had been the first to reveal the secret. What then?

The lights in the dormer were out. From many beds came the sound of steady breathing. But for Podger there came no blessed repose. Staring at the starlight on the low, beamed ceiling, he allowed, without meaning to, his imagination to blossom.

A thought struck him; for the implication was simple and obvious: was the South American playing these tricks on him in order that he should in fact seek another Study? To drive him away from Room Six, so that he could continue his mysterious 'studying' undisturbed?

It might well be. So simple was this explanation that Podger felt a sense of victory within him. His clever, astute brain, ever sharpened by his own intelligent thoughts, had picked upon the truth, as straight as an arrow. So the new kid had been ignorant of the fact that in Study Six there was an amateur detective far superior in his powers of complex deductions to any fictional figure.

It was when Podger was dozing off, his fears vanished in this new mood of self-confidence, that something roused him to a new wakefulness. For a moment he stared at the ceiling, trying to discover what sound he had heard; then it came again.

Someone, somewhere, was leaving his bed, stealthily.

6

MISTAKEN IDENTITY

MR. HARRISON closed his door and turned left along the passage. He walked quietly, and was even wearing rubber-soled shoes; for it was in the region of 11 p.m., and Monks' Court slept – or the more youthful portion of it.

Mr. Harrison, who presided over classes in geology and mineralogy, was not also in charge of astronomy: simply because there was no such subject in the School curriculum. Had there been, he would assuredly have been the choice of the Headmaster, Dr. Ransome, for the honour of dispensing the necessary learning, information and instruction. For the subject of astronomy was Mr. Harrison's hobby: he was, in fact, no mean amateur astronomer.

In slight recognition of his reputation in this interesting field, Dr. Ransome had placed at Mr. Harrison's personal disposal one of the highest turrets of Monks' Court. It was from there, these days (or rather these nights), that the geology master looked out at the star-bright cosmos, through his astronomer's telescope.

The night was quiet. The moon was waning, and its last light was beginning to slant dimly through the tall, mullioned windows that faced the Study doors on the other flank of the passage. There was the calm almost of sunshine here in this moonlit place; it was as though the sun's warmth lay still on the moss-deep tiles, the mellow walls, the stained-glass windows.

Turning the corner at the end of the corridor, he was about to climb the first flight of steps that would ultimately bring him to the high and remote turret, when a sound caught his ears, and he stopped immediately.

It had been something like the click of a latch.

Ahead of him there was nothing to be seen. Behind him was the corner of the passage. Beyond the corner?

He retraced his quiet steps a few paces, and stood on the corner, looking back along the great length of the passage where ran the row of Studies. The first shafts of the dying moonlight were creeping round the ramparts of the roofs, and slanted, pale and tranquil, across the passage.

There seemed nothing untoward. Yet Mr. Harrison was sure that he had heard the definite click of a lock or a latch. True, a hasp might have been left half-shot by one of the boys on his way up to dormer; and now, in the silence of the warm night, the settling of this ancient building had moved the lock; and it had clicked. Perhaps.

Mr. Harrison walked quietly down the passage, in the direction whence he had just come. But from behind not one of the Study doors did there issue any further indications of a late prowler. Mr. Harrison, making scarcely a sound in his rubber-soled shoes, went on to the end of the passage, walking slowly; listening carefully; his eyes alert.

.   .   .   .   .

Podger Horatio Pomeroy Pepys blinked in the darkness.

He had followed del Pino easily enough along the passage from Long Dormer, and down the stairs, but now the kid had either put a spurt on, or was suspicious that he was being followed, and therefore hiding in some recess or alcove here in the gloomiest part of the West wing.

Horatio P. deliberated. He preferred to think that the former supposition was correct: that del Pino had put on a little more speed, and was away upon his nefarious business in some other precinct. For the alternative was distasteful to Podger: that del Pino had stopped, suspicious, and was hiding in the shadows to prove or disprove his guess that he was being tracked. If his follower were now to walk on, the new kid would be very likely to spring when the time was ripe.

The memory of the ivory-handled knife came back to the mind of the lurking Pepys; and he swallowed.

It was when he was struggling to make up his mind to push onwards in the hope of catching the scent again that a sound came to his fat and super-attentive ears.

A sound like the click of a lock or a latch.

He jumped. Silent as the building was, the sound might have issued from many yards distant; but in the gloom it had startled the watcher. He knew now, however, a great deal more than he had known a moment before. That noise had, without any doubt, come from the corridor where the Fourth Form Studies lay. It was, as like as not, the click of a Study door. So del Pino, not content with being in Study Six after dormer roll-call and on Sunday afternoon, was now visiting that room in the depths of the night, when the rest of the School was fast asleep!

Sherlock Pepys blinked keenly into the gloom. He had already deduced that there was something in that Study that was claiming every possible part of del Pino's attention. Now the matter was doubly proved. The new kid, in fact, seemed to have the greatest difficulty in keeping *away* from his Study, even for a moment.

He reached the corner. Already he could glimpse the dull, ghostly sheen of the moonlight that came dreaming through the many-paned casements. Already he could see this same moonglow gleaming upon the handle of a nearby door.

What he could not see was Mr. Harrison.

Mr. Harrison was at this moment reaching the end of the corridor, walking with quiet and caution. He had passed all the doors of the Studies but the last one; and from none of them had he heard any sound. He would try the last one in the row, and then retrace his steps, to dismiss the strange clicking sound as that of a settling timber and to resume his former journey to the turret where his telescope awaited him. So that, in this instant, Mr. Harrison was progressing towards the corner just beyond which Podger Pepys was also walking, as stealthy and as cautious as the geology master.

It did.

Mr. Harrison, an intelligent, unexcitable man, was not startled very severely by the sudden exclamation in the gloom ahead of him; but he was alarmed, instinctively. On the other hand, Podger Pepys, being neither intelligent nor unexcitable, was palpably petrified.

They met.

With a fierce hoot of terror, the portly prowler deemed it his best plan to throw himself full-tilt and notwithstanding at whatever enemy had chosen to seek him out at this awful and nocturnal moment.

'*Oooch!*' gasped Mr. Harrison, caught in the midriff by a large, powerful head.

'*Hooops!*' hooted Podger, as his opponent went pitching over backwards beneath this Pepysian avalanche. Together they hit the parquet floor and there rolled, struggling; squirmed, twisting and turning; battled, hitting and missing; and generally created such a confusion that the passage was loud with their strife. So much so that even now, only a few seconds after the first shock of the encounter, voices were raised in the dormitories:

'Come on, you chaps – burglars!'

'What's the din?'

'Rally round – a fight!'

'Come on, you men – there's a fire!'

And, as the redoubtable Mr. Harrison struggled

with his unseen, unknown opponent in the passage, and the terrified Pepys battled with his unseen, unknown opponent in the passage, the School awoke: and within minutes was racing to the scene.

.　　.　　.　　　.

The lights burned cheerfully; there was the companionable hum of voices. Within the interested ring of fellows – and there must have been at least thirty or forty of them – sat Mr. Harrison. Tousled, tattered, and panting for breath, he gazed around him, as though undecided for a moment as to his own identity. Then he saw the boy who sat beside him: and he realized, from his worn-and-torn condition, that this must be his opponent, hitherto unseen.

'Del Pino!' snapped Mr. Harrison.

Del Pino, with his pyjamas tattered and his dressing-gown torn, surveyed Mr. Harrison darkly. Neither of them was aware that, not far away, a third bedraggled figure was standing among the gaping crowd of fellows. And this third person was not anxious to acquaint anyone that a mistake had been made; and that his identity had been exchanged, by the most happy and fortuitous circumstances, with that of another – by name del Pino.

'Del Pino!' said Mr. Harrison, accepting the assistance of Jim Raymond's hand to enable himself to rise. 'What are you doing out of your dormitory?'

'I'm sorry, sir,' said the new chap, standing up and rubbing one ear that was still ringing from a chance blow.

'I've no doubt you are sorry,' nodded the astronomer, brushing himself down as best he might; 'I would go so far as to hazard the guess that you will be even sorrier in the morning. Kindly report to me immediately after Prayers, in my Study.' He looked round, indignantly. 'You others – get back to your beds at once!'

'Are you hurt, sir?' asked Jim Raymond, as Mr. Harrison straightened his gown. It was partly his flowing gown that had given Podger to think of ghoulies and ghosties when they had met so precipitately. Mr. Harrison, who loved it as his favourite garb, had slipped it on for his session in the turret-observatory: and Podger had glimpsed its black and flowing folds and had seen them – through the spectacles of his powerful imagination – as the great wings of a monster bat.

'I am *not* hurt, thank you, Raymond. However, that was no fault of del Pino's. Did you know he was out of your dormitory?'

'I was asleep, sir. I woke up when you began kicking up that colossal shindy – I mean when we heard you being – er – attacked.'

'Quite so, Raymond. See that the dormitory resumes its normal function. Good night, Raymond. Good night, boys.'

A small, muted chorus of 'good nights' followed the retreating figure of the outraged geology master; then Jim and his three friends began their return journey to Long Dormer, more slowly than they had come.

'Did any of you men know del Pino was out of the dormer?' asked Jim, as they climbed the stairs.

'I was asleep,' said Gregory, yawning.

'I was unconscious, old bean,' said Dresley.

'I was out to the wide,' nodded Bob Mayfield.

Jim Raymond shrugged.

'If that new man keeps things up at this rate,' he said seriously, 'he won't be at Monks' Court very long.'

'Which will make things a heap more peaceful all round,' declared Gregory Stevens; and the Quartet got back into their beds.

This time there were only two who did not sleep immediately.

Del Pino had a painful ear and was burning with fury.

Podger Pepys had two painful ears, a black eye, some skin off his shoulder and a bruised foot: but otherwise he was perfectly happy, for Mr. Harrison had not known who had given him such punishment in that darkened passage. Podger Horatio Pomeroy Pepys had, in point of fact, hurled himself at a master with his head down, had clipped that master's ear, had socked his august and majestic jaw – and had got clean away with it except for the more obvious signs of battle!

7

PODGER THE PUGILIST

'HELLO, Podgy – what have you been doing, box-ing with a steamroller bigger than yourself?'

Pepys glowered.

'Well, well, well! Pepys looks a bit bent this morning!'

Pepys blinked with his one sound eye, indignantly.

The fellows trooped into the classroom; and with-in a few moments the opportunity of ragging the battered buffoon was gone; yet his appearance still excited much quiet interest.

The fellows in Long Dormer had got over the first shock of seeing their portly mascot earlier this morning. He had awakened with them, and, with them, had risen from his bed, as would a water-buffalo arise from his murky pool after a midnight fight with ten elephants.

'I just give it up,' Jim Raymond had said, after they had failed to discover how Pepys had achieved his surprising appearance. 'He went to bed last night looking perfectly fit.'

'In prime condition,' nodded Gregory.

'And this morning,' went on Jim seriously, 'he gets up looking like a prize-fighter!'

'Or a double dahlia in a high wind,' agreed Gregory.

'The question *is*,' muttered Bob, 'who was the bloke he battled with? You don't get a black eye and a chip off your chin simply by falling down the stairs or crossing the road without looking.'

The Company of Four was mystified; and it was still pondering the problem of the portly and pugilistic Podge when the first class began. So were the other fellows. To every eye it was clear that if a fellow got into *that* state there must have been another fellow to hit him. Who was the other fellow?

In the dormer, when the Quartet had surrounded Podger and asked him with deep interest how he had managed to look so second-hand this morning, his answer had been both ready and untruthful (for the last thing he wished to do was to admit he had struck Mr. Harrison – or that Mr. Harrison had struck him):

'I – I went sleep-walking and f-fell down the stairs!'

'Sure it wasn't up them?' queried Bob, disbelievingly.

'I'm – I mean I slipped up in the b-bath and hit my head on the tap!'

'That's funny – the taps aren't broken anywhere in the bathrooms!'

And now the persecuted Pomeroy had a further inquirer to answer. Before the class had been assembled more than a few minutes, Mr. Jackersby had noticed the strange and sorry condition of Podger's countenance.

'Pepys!'

'Oh! Y-yes, sir?'

'Have you been fighting?'

'F-f-fighting, sir?'

'Have you been employed in fisticuffs?' nodded Mr. Jackersby.

'Oh no, sir! I – I m-mean y-yes, sir! Er – fisti – *what*, sir?'

'Pepys, have you been *fighting*? Isn't that a simple enough question?'

'Y-yes, sir!'

'You have?'

'N-no, sir! I m-mean yes, sir, it's a s-simple enough question.'

'Pepys!'

'Oh l-lawks!'

'With whom have you been fighting?' snapped the Housemaster of Winston.

'With Mr. Harrison, sir! I mean—'

'*What?*'

'I mean with D-Dr. Ransome, sir! Th-that is to say I haven't been fighting at all, sir!'

'How, then,' pursued Mr. Jackersby, 'did your visage achieve that remarkable state of decay?'

A roar of merriment went up.

'Cease!' thundered Mr. Jackersby. 'Pepys, answer!'

'I – I – I f-fell d-down the stairs, sir, and hit my head on the taps!'

'*What?*'

'I s-slipped in the b-bath, sir, and c-caught my head on the b-banisters!'

'*Pepys!* Come to me after class!'

'Oh, yes, s-sir.'

The lesson was resumed, though not for some moments, during which Mr. Jackersby was obliged to allow time for the Fourth Formers to recover their gravity.

But, even to the portly prevaricator of Four-B, the events of the previous night were by no means crystal clear. He had been struggling as a demon demented with the huge shadowy monster bat that had swooped upon him from the rafters of the corridor, and had been milling into it with a determination to escape its noisome clutches alive, when he had seized the opportunity of slipping free of the enemy's steely talons; and had done so, to flee along the passage, speechless with terror, heading for the dormitory. But long before he reached it the other fellows had come clattering down the stairs; and the discomfited Podge had willy-nilly gone back with them – to find Mr. Harrison sitting on the floor of the passage with del Pino. Both torn and much distressed.

Now, during Pepys's battle with his opponent, his imagination had permitted his visualizing a monster bat, or perhaps a dozen Zombies armed to the teeth. But now, in the clarity of the electric light and the common sense of slower reasoning, Podger Pepys had been forced to face the fact that it must have been one of these two whom he had fought: and, come to remember, the *voice* of the monster-Zombie had sounded very like that of the geology master's.

Then where had del Pino come from? In a moment, Podger Pepys—or, rather, Sexton Pepys, the sleuth with the radar brain—had realized the secret of the matter. Within a moment of his escape from Mr. Harrison, del Pino had come out of the Study where Sherlock Pepys had been tracking him, and had sought to slip past the strugglers and make his way to the dormer before the whole School was wakened—and he was found missing from his bed—hoping to leave the combatants locked in their death-struggle. But Mr. Harrison, perhaps shooting out a hand or kicking with his foot, intent upon wounding his assailant, had wounded del Pino: and within an instant the new boy had become involved in a battle hitherto private. In the heat of the moment, the girth of this new contestant had not struck Mr. Harrison as being different and slightly smaller than that of the old. He had continued the good fight, with all his might: and it was del Pino who had suffered the final furies of the outraged geology master's rage.

Thus it was that, although Podger Pepys was experiencing some little bother this morning, what with questions and Mr. Jackersby's own and more authoritative inquiry, he was nevertheless safe from the accusation that was being at this moment levelled at del Pino's head. Del Pino had attacked a master of Monks' Court School; and no one would ever know that it had been P. H. P. Pepys who had delivered the greater damage to that majestic personage. He could therefore bear amiably with the questioning of his fellows, and the inquiry directed at him by his Housemaster.

Within fifteen minutes there was a tap on the door of Mr. Jackersby's classroom, and del Pino entered.

'Late, del Pino?'

'I had to see Mr. Harrison after Prayers, sir.'

'And did you see him?'

'Yes, sir.'

'Very well. Take your place.'

But, as the new boy sat down at his desk with not a glance to right or left, Mr. Jackersby did not put him to the same questioning as he had directed towards Pepys. Del Pino was in a plight as bad as Pepys's, as regard their countenances; but Mr. Jackersby had been one of the first to arrive on the scene last night, and he knew how del Pino had obtained his ripening eye.

At break, the Company of Four met together in the Quadrangle, there to discuss the amazing events of the night.

'That man del Pino's going to be up for the high jump,' said Bob Mayfield, 'if he doesn't look out.'

'He's been out of bounds twice so far,' nodded Gregory Stevens, 'and now spends his nights socking the beaks!'

Jim Raymond looked ruminative as they strolled in the warm sunshine towards the cricket pavilion.

'It's pretty obvious he's got something in his Study that interests him a good deal, since he can never tear himself away from the place. He was obviously down there last night, and Old Harry disturbed him.'

'Well, well, well!' chuckled Bob, as a familiar form rolled ponderously within view.

'Ass!' hooted Pepys.

'Poor old Podge,' grinned Gregory, 'fell down the stairs and slipped on the bath-mat!'

'Slipped in the bath,' said Dresley Burgess, 'and fell flat on his back on the stair-carpet!'

'Say what you like,' shrugged Podger Pepys, 'so long as it amuses you.' He gave a sudden, knowing wink. 'I must say poor old Harrison is looking a bit cut-up this morning, what?'

'So would you be, if del Pino laid into you,' said Jim Raymond, eyeing him closely.

'Del Pino?' asked Podger. 'He couldn't hurt a fly. It's quite obvious to me that it was someone else who began that fight. A big, strapping fellow who knew how to use his fists.'

'Such as?' queried Dresley quietly.

'No names,' said Podger, shaking his head with a confidential leer of one good eye. 'But it must have been some muscular chap who knew how to box with the best of 'em.'

'Why are you so certain,' asked Jim Raymond gently, 'that someone else attacked Old Harry, *as well* as del Pino?'

'I'm not at all certain, my dear Raymond. It's merely obvious. When a fellow my size goes pitching into a beak, he makes his mark, I can tell you!'

'A fellow – *your* size?'

'Well, I – I mean a big fellow. He must have been a big fellow, to have . . .' But already the boastful Podge was veering away from the groups of chaps, his voice trailing off ineffectually.

'Just a minute, Podge!' called Jim Raymond.

'Can't stop!'

'Podger, you fat falsifier!'

'Sorry – see you in form!'

And before Jim Raymond and his friends could pursue the Fourth Former whose recent words had so piqued their curiosity, the bell began ringing from the turrets; and there was a general trek back into the classrooms. As Jim climbed the steps from the Quad, a Third Former clutched his arm.

'Mr. Jackersby wants you in his Study, Raymond, first thing after morning school!'

'All right, kid, thanks.'

'What now?' grunted Bob Mayfield as they opened their desks and sorted over their primers.

'Who knows?' shrugged Jim. But as he sat down, and silence descended over the class, he was thinking less about his coming interview with the Housemaster of Winston than of some of the things Podger Pepys had said a few minutes ago in the Quadrangle. Podger knew more than he would say about the attack upon Mr. Harrison. But before long, if Jim Raymond had his way, Podger would say all he knew.

With the coming of del Pino to Monks' Court there had also come an atmosphere of mystery and uneasiness. If Pepys knew anything that would help clear things up, then he must tell. Or be made to.

8

INQUISITION IN STUDY SIX

'WELL, del Pino?'

'I have to apologize, sir.'

'Doubtless. But I have asked you here to give me something more than your apology. An explanation.'

The master and the boy, who had only a few hours ago been struggling upon the floor of the upper corridor, hitting and shouting, were now slightly more composed. There was indeed a more perceptible dignity in this second encounter.

'It – was my window, sir. I remembered I had left it wide open, and went down to fasten it.'

Mr. Harrison waited. He was wise enough to know that a boy tied himself in knots more quickly – if he were lying – when left uninterrupted in his story than when prompted and helped along. Silence embarrasses a liar. Yet, if this rule were true, the explanation of del Pino's was also true, for he showed no embarrassment when Mr. Harrison offered nothing but attentive silence.

'On my way down to close the window,' the new boy from South America continued, 'I rounded the first corner after the main staircase – and bumped right into you, sir.'

Silence from Mr. Harrison. But the words flowed easily:

'As you can believe, I was startled out of my wits, and hit out at once.' (Mr. Harrison stroked his jaw, very gently.) 'The thought of burglars was on my mind at the time, for I had come down to close the window for that very purpose: that no burglar should find an easy way in. Before I was able to realize it was one of our masters I was hitting, I had used my fists too readily. I am sorry, sir.'

At last Mr. Harrison broke his silence.

'So am I, del Pino. I shall, in fact, continue to be sorry until my jaw ceases to ache. Did you not know that the prefects of this House make a nightly tour of inspection to ensure that all windows and doors are fastened?'

'No, sir.'

'Well, they do. If you forget a window in future – remember the prefects, and go to sleep. Now, del Pino, are you sure you have given me the absolute truth?'

'But of course, sir! Why should I lie?'

'There could be a thousand reasons,' murmured Mr. Harrison drily, 'and all of them utterly different. However, I am going to accept your story. The Headmaster, Dr. Ransome, has asked me to make a full inquiry into the – er – disturbance of last night; and if I am satisfied with the explanation, then it must satisfy the Headmaster. That is why I wish to be particularly careful in finding the absolute truth of this matter.'

Del Pino waited patiently, in silence, his feet together and his hands behind him at ease.

'You have assured me that your explanation is the truth,' went on the geology master. 'I shall accept that.'

Del Pino tapped on the door of the classroom, entered, and sat down at his desk after explaining to Mr. Jackersby why he was late. The episode was closed. The disturbance in the corridor late last night had been investigated, and would now be relegated to the past. Del Pino had had his warning, and for that he was grateful, even though it had cost him a bruised ear. His warning was that he must keep clear of the fat meddler Pepys, whose curiosity was becoming dangerous.

Morning class continued.

At the end of it, Jim Raymond went, as he had been bid, to see Mr. Jackersby, Housemaster of Winston.

'It is about ten minutes to luncheon,' said the athletic mathematician, when Jim had closed the door of the Study. 'Therefore I shall keep you no longer than both our robust appetites would wish.'

As Raymond gave a quick grin, 'Jacko' dropped the levity of his tone, and talked quickly.

'Raymond, what about this new boy, del Pino?'

'I believe Mr. Harrison is dealing with that matter, sir.'

'Yes, yes, I know – it was Mr. Harrison's black eye,

and therefore his privilege to investigate its cause. But I mean what about the other things?'

Jim looked puzzled.

'Other things, sir?'

'Now look here, Raymond, I know it isn't your habit to tell tales about any of the fellows; but the fact remains that you've been having trouble with del Pino. Haven't you?'

After a short silence Jim said briefly:

'He's new here, sir.'

'M'm. Why does he keep to his Study, do you know?'

'I understand he's swotting something, sir.'

'Ah. What, exactly? Does he say?'

'I've no idea, sir.'

Mr. Jackersby shrugged, turning away and pacing the small, richly-panelled Study.

'Raymond, I am responsible for Winston House. You, as the Head Boy of the Fourth, are one of my officers. Del Pino is in the indirect charge of both of us, and is our responsibility – particularly yours, because you are closer to him and to his activities, at work, in the dormitory and the dining-hall. In other words, Raymond, you act for me and you report to me when this sort of thing happens among the members of your Form. You can do that without losing comradeship with your fellows.'

He stopped pacing, looked quickly at his watch, and finished:

'Do what you can for del Pino. Sort him out. Find out what his problem is. Do all you can, but if it's too hard, come to me. All right?'

'Not quite, sir.'

Mr. Jackersby raised his brows with a jerk.

'What part of it is wrong, then?'

'No part, sir. I'll do all you ask and be glad to. If I can help a new kid to find his feet I enjoy doing it, because first Term at a new school can be hard on a chap. What I would like to know, sir, is who sneaked on him?'

'Sneaked?'

'Most of the House, if not the whole School, has heard about last night's episode involving del Pino. But I've had only two other instances of the kid's proving awkward, and I certainly didn't report them.'

A slow smile played on the lean mouth of the mathematician for a moment.

'It's high time you learned, my dear Raymond, that we "beaks" – as you little devils call us – get to know about many more things than those few that are reported. There are no concealed microphones or trick-television sets in Monks' Court – but masters are human, and humans have eyes and ears – and also brains, contrary to the general belief of the pupils. You just take it from me that although I happen to know a little more about del Pino than you think, it isn't because anyone "sneaked". You've my word for that. Now go and have a good lunch.'

'Sacked?' asked Gregory Stevens, as Jim took his chair at the dining-table.

'Whacked?' asked Bob Mayfield, passing the salt.

'Neither,' he told them. 'Jacko just asked me to keep an eye on the new kid, del Pino.'

'What are you?' queried Dres Burgess, 'honorary fellow of the Pupils' Wet-nursing Society?'

'There are more ways of helping a new kid than by wiping his nose for him,' grunted Jim.

'Yers,' nodded Bob, 'you can always bash it.'

'Exactly. If he takes kindly to treatment, he can have my good advice. If he's a hard-and-fast rebel, he can have my fist.'

.   .   .   .   .

Horatio Pomeroy Pepys, Pride of the House of Podge, sat in his Study, alone.

This, for him, was a strange occupation, since he was not stealing, hiding, or eating tuck. During any one of those three pursuits one might be certain to find the Friar Tuck of the Fourth utterly alone and private with his purloined provender. But at all other times he was wont to prove himself a gregarious animal, and sought the company of any who could stand his presence. And if they chanced to be enjoying a little feast of their own, his arrival would be almost a certainty; for Podge was possessed of a proboscis peculiarly designed for the prime purpose of discovering tuck.

He blinked impatiently, and tapped his foot as he sat reclining and cross-legged, in the most comfortable armchair in the room. There was of course a good reason for his lonely vigil. The reason was called del Pino. Though Podger Pepys still nursed a painful eye, an aching foot, a lump on his head and a grazed shoulder, he now regarded himself as something of a

74

fighter. Had he not taken on a full-grown master, and given him punishment fit to remember for days, only last night?

Thus inflated with his own esteem, and confident that, after this demonstration of his powers, he could easily fell that new kid with a blow – nay, a single glance – he waited in Study Six for del Pino. He was jolly well going to ask him what he jolly well meant by practically sleeping in this Study. On Sunday afternoons, after roll-call at dormer, even when all the other fellows were in bed, del Pino had been found down here. Why? Podger wished to know. It was, after all, his own Study, as well as that South American kid's.

'Answer me!' said Podger sternly and aloud, casting a steely eye (his other was rather ripe) at the shivering form of the new boy. 'Come along now – no nonsense, or I shall have to teach you a little lesson, my friend!'

But del Pino did not appear for his dire punishment. Had he done so, of course, it was just conceivable that he would have tweaked the belligerent nose of H. Pomeroy so soundly that the yelp would have been audible in the nearest village. But the clash of wills was not, it seemed, to be put to the test. There was no footstep immediately outside the door, as yet. There came no new kid to shiver at the sight of the great Pepys, mighty in his majestic wrath.

Podger was just going through the delightful rehearsal of tempering justice with mercy, and commanding the new kid to rise from his knees and stop shivering so violently, when there came the tap on the door that he had been awaiting so long.

'Come!' he called authoritatively. 'Come!'

The door opened.

'Hello, Podger!'

'Greetings, little bulldozer!'

'How now, Friar Pilferer of Tuck!'

'Salutations, my slender little sea-elephant!'

The Company of Four trooped in.

'Now look here, you kids,' rapped out Podger peremptorily, 'you'd better cut, before I chuck you out, I'm busy.'

'Podger,' said Jim Raymond quietly, 'there's something I want to ask you.'

'I simply haven't time, my dear Raymond. Cut along now, there's a good chap.'

'I want to ask you,' went on the Leader of the Quartet, 'what you meant this morning when you talked about a chap *your* size pitching into Old Harry.'

'Oh, d-dear. Oh, I say, you c-can't come in here asking a l-lot of silly questions, Raymond, as if you . . .'

'Podger, relax.' And Jim closed the door. 'Now then,' he said gently.

'Oh, m-my hat! L-look here, I – oh, crumbs!'

The grand inquisition was on: but it was the portly Podge who was going to do the shivering.

9

THE ABSENTEE

'I TELL you, I don't know anything about it!'

'Come along, Podgy!'

'B-but I wasn't there! Even if I was, it was too dark to see anything! I – I mean . . .'

'So it was too dark to see, was it?'

Jim Raymond fixed the portly captive with a steady gaze. Podger squirmed. He had been sitting here, quite innocently waiting for that idiot del Pino, and now these asses had come barging in and messing up the programme.

'I'll trouble you to leave my Study!' he hooted indignantly.

'Can't,' grinned Bob Mayfield, 'it's too much trouble.'

'You've admitted you were there in the corridor, Podger,' cut in Jim Raymond. 'Now all we want to know is why you were there.'

'I wasn't there at all! I was fast asleep, and as soon as I heard the shindy I just hit out as hard as I – I mean I just woke up and—'

'You hit out, Podger, and then—?'

'If you think I'm going to admit I socked a beak, Raymond, you're quite mistaken! That sort of thing is frowned upon at Monks' Court!'

'Listen, Podger,' he said. 'I know now that you got mixed up in that scrap in the corridor. You can have my word that it won't get past us. Have we ever reported you for any of your crazy escapades in the past, once we've given our word that we won't?'

'N-no, but—'

'Then you can trust us. All I want is to find out what's bothering del Pino. He's got to be straightened up before he has the whole of Winston upset. Now: can you help me, by telling us what you were doing last night?'

'I'm not sure I can,' said Podger Pepys warily. 'Not at all sure.' He eyed the Quartet cautiously from the depths of his chair. 'That depends on how much it's – I mean how much I'm able to.'

'One meat pie,' murmured Greg Stevens.

'Two apple fritters,' suggested Dres Burgess.

'Three cream buns,' added Bob Mayfield.

'If he won't give me the information,' frowned Jim Raymond, 'I'm not buying it. He can go and bury himself.'

'Really, Raymond, I never for a moment suggested that you should buy information! It was your corrupt confederates who implicated that allusion – I mean inculcated that confusion!'

'Well, Podger?' asked Jim Raymond quietly.

'I – I was following del Pino,' admitted Pepys. 'He left the dormer and I went after him. Then Old

Harry leapt at me from the shadows with a great knife in his hand—'

'With a *what*?'

'I mean a penknife—'

'Trying to poison you with it!' nodded Dres Burgess.

'Exactly! No, you ass, I mean he—'

'And where was del Pino?' put in Jim.

'I never saw him. I was as surprised as anyone when I came back with the rest of the chaps and saw Harrison sitting there with del Pino looking like New Year's Eve after the party!'

Jim Raymond nodded slowly.

'Obviously he was in here again,' he said. 'You and Mr. Harrison met each other, and when del Pino heard the din he tried to slip past in the corridor before he was found.'

'And got mixed up in the fight,' added Dres Burgess.

Gregory nodded. 'I thought old Podge couldn't have done that much damage to poor old Harry.'

'Well, really, Stevens! I might tell you I managed to give quite a considerable account of myself!'

'Ye-es,' conceded Gregory, 'I suppose thirty-four stone of solid Pepys *would* make quite an impression on a thin geology master.'

'Where's del Pino now?' asked Jim seriously.

'I'm waiting for him, Raymond. I wish to have a word with him – in private.'

'Can't we be invited, Podgy?' asked Bob Mayfield, looking hurt.

'My dear Mayfield, you have a Study of your own.

79

Rather overcrowded, with the four of you there, I agree; but you must remember that privacy should be inviolable. I must therefore request you all to leave.'

'What a pity,' sighed Gregory; 'what a *shame*!'

'And we were thinking of bringing all that – er – stuff along, too,' nodded Dresley, 'so that we could make ourselves comfortable while we were waiting for del Pino.'

'S-stuff?' asked Podger quickly.

'Oh well,' said Dresley, with a sad shake of his head, 'if Podger doesn't want to share our little spread. I must say we shouldn't force him.'

'S-s-spread?' panted Pepys, piqued.

'Privacy,' said Bob Mayfield heavily, going to the door, 'must remain in a violet-bowl, as dear Podge so rightly says.'

Jim Raymond perched himself on the edge of a chair, prepared to wait for the missing Fourth Former.

'But my dear fellows,' beamed Podger hospitably, 'I had no idea you wanted to come to – er – tea with me! Please make yourselves thoroughly at home! I'm afraid I've not much in my cupboard, but – but perhaps you could help me out with a thing or two?'

His eyes were bright with the unholy light of appetite. His cheeks became shiny with expectation.

Jim Raymond's serious expression broke into a grin.

'It's going to break my heart if we let the idiot starve now,' he said. 'Go and see what we've got, would you, Greg?'

Gregory made for the door.

'Really, Raymond, I suppose you think I've invited you here for a modest spread simply because I heard you m-mention t-tuck?'

'I certainly do,' smiled Jim.

'Oh. Then you're a mean-minded b-beast! I mean you're kind, to say the least. And very welcome, of course, to whatever small repast I can offer you.'

And Podger Pepys, the perfect and shining host, sat enthroned in his armchair, inviting the three fellows of Study Four to make themselves comfortable, while Gregory Stevens fetched what he could discover in their own cupboard.

Within a few minutes of his return the feast was under way. It lasted until their 'host' had completed his inroads into the provender – that is to say about ten minutes – and finally they sat back to wait for del Pino.

Del Pino did not come.

Jim Raymond went up to call the dormer-roll with a puzzled brow. The two Fourth Forms were assembled, for the most part sleepily, for the summer night was warm. The roll was called, and there was only one absentee. His name was del Pino.

As Jim got undressed he talked in low tones to his three friends.

'Ever since the kid's been here he's stuck to his Study like a clam to a rock – and just when we're trying to ask him what game he's playing he shoots off into the limbo.'

'And even breaks roll-call,' nodded Dresley, mystified.

'Going to send his name in as absent?' asked Gregory, putting his gym shoes handy near the bed.

'No. If he's back by the morning we'll keep quiet.' Jim glanced at the soft shoes that Gregory had placed ready. 'You going to break bounds tonight or something?'

'I'm breaking dormer,' Gregory nodded, 'but not the grounds. You can come along, if it interests you.'

'What's on the programme, Greg?' Dresley asked, knowing that Stevens's escapades were sometimes amusing.

'You can come with me if you like,' was all he received by way of reply. 'It's up to you.'

'All right, I'm game.'

'I'll stay in my bed,' grunted Bob. 'I like my full night's snooze.'

Ten minutes later, Mr. Jackersby came along to the dormer to put the lights out.

'Everything is in order, Raymond?' he asked from the doorway.

'Yes, sir.'

'Very well. Good night, boys!'

The lights flicked out as a muffled chorus of 'good nights' rose from the beds.

'You didn't tell him what sort of order everything was in,' muttered Dresley, as Jim put his head on the pillow.

'Well, he didn't ask me that.'

Across on the other side of the long dormitory, Podger Pepys dozed off, still happily replete from the feast in his own Study. Jim Raymond lay wakeful for some time, wondering why del Pino had not been to his Study during the evening, and wondering whether he would be back by morning. Bob Mayfield gave a mighty grunt of healthy contentment as he turned over and prepared to emit gargantuan snores. From Dresley's bed a whisper floated.

'Greg . . .'

'M'm?'

'When do we start?'

'As soon as the beaks and prefects have gone their rounds. Don't want to get nabbed.'

So, for another fifteen minutes or so, during which the expectant Dresley found himself hard put to it to remain awake, there was silence in Long Dormer. Then:

'Dresley . . . you ready?'

'Yes. Are you?'

'Yes. Don't make a row.'

They slid from their beds and laced their gym shoes.

10

THE FLYING BUBBLE

It was Mr. Harrison, the geology master and keen amateur astronomer, who was the first to witness the Flying Bubble.

This, at least, was the name given to it by the first few people who saw it; and in point of fact it was an apt title. On this particular night, when Dresley Burgess and Gregory Stevens were out on their mysterious errand, Mr. Harrison was studying the stellar map of the night sky, from the lofty turret lent to him for the purpose. The moon was on the wane, and the air was warm – almost stifling, although a slow breeze was shifting idly across the ancient battlements of the massive buildings.

With the lens adjusted to 'short' distance – a distance which, however, had still to be reckoned in light-years, so great was it – Mr. Harrison moved the sights across the great mass of the Milky Way, and focused upon Mars, that strange, speculative planet whose history and geography has interested many generations of astronomers, whose 'canals' showed sometimes with startling clarity, and whose polar caps of ice gave credence to the idea that it was this ice that flowed, during Mars's 'summer', into the 'canals', thus darkening their lines.

Mr. Harrison stared. Across his restricted field of vision there now, suddenly, drifted another body, an alien shape; and for one breath-taking instant he imagined that some planet or some star had moved in the firmament, and was heading towards the gleaming Mars. The idea lasted but a moment. To the trained eye of this astronomer it became clear now that the new heavenly body was not a cloud of nebulae, thousands of light-years distant, but a much nearer phenomenon. It floated, indeed, only a few hundred feet in the air above the tumbled, slumbering buildings of the School.

The shape that drifted across his lens was spherical. It was also semi-transparent. And beneath it there was suspended a dark shape as that of a small black box. For perhaps ten minutes this strange apparition drifted within sight of the turret, southwards across Banner Wood and beyond; then its queer, grey semi-transparency rendered it gradually invisible even to the highly magnifying lens of the telescope.

'Strange . . .' he murmured, talking to himself as men do who work in solitude or in the still of night. 'Very strange indeed . . .' And in a moment he was back with Mars, adjusting the lens and then observing, taking notes on a small pad beside his instrument. The planet was particularly clear tonight, and many of its markings were revealed with a fascinating sharpness of pattern.

Mr. Harrison gazed, and, gazing, forgot about the Flying Bubble.

It was by the slightest chance that he was not privileged to observe a second flying phenomenon this night; for, at this moment, two Fourth Formers were standing in the north-west corner of the deserted Quadrangle, and with them was a large, complicated-looking kite.

'Where's the wind?' asked Dresley, as his crack-brained friend prepared his mechanical child for flight.

'What little there is,' murmured Gregory, 'is nor'-west.'

'Is there enough to lift it?'

'Didn't you see it flying yesterday in South Meadow?'

'I was forgetting,' nodded Dresley, 'it goes up even if you breathe on it.'

'It does,' said its proud operator, and looked round the sky. From near the hill-rims came the wan light of the dying moon. There were no clouds, and the heavens were splashed with stars in their high, glinting millions.

'Where d'you want me to stand?' asked Dresley, as a humble member of this historic experiment.

Gregory did not answer.

'Where do you want me to—?' began Burgess again; then he noticed his friend was gazing skywards, as though puzzled.

'What's up, Greggy?'

'That's funny. Thought I saw a light—'

'Where?'

'In the window of that turret – look! There it is again!'

Dresley peered. It was true enough. A faint gleam of light was winking in the tiny window – scarcely greater than an arrow-slit – of the turret at the end of the West wing.

'You know who *that* is,' said Dresley.

'Who?'

'Old Harry, with his spy-glass.'

'You're very ignorant, Burgess, for your age.'

'Is that so? Well, I must say—'

'You should know that Old Harry's observatory is in the turret round the angle of the wing – out of sight from where we are here. It's above the San.'

'Oh, that's different.'

'I should just say it is,' nodded Gregory softly. 'Who can be flitting about up there at this time of night?'

'Dres,' murmured the kite-fiend, 'that wants looking into.'

'Agreed,' nodded his friend briefly. The same sense of excitement gripped them both. Monks' Court slept; yet up there the light gleamed. What hand had lit the flame? Whose eyes saw by its light?

'Come on!' said Gregory, and lifted his super-kite clear of the ground, carrying it carefully as they made their way to the small window beside the West door that had provided their egress a few minutes ago. Dresley was through first, and turned round to take the kite from Gregory, when the latter stopped him. His voice came softly:

'Well – I'm – jiggered—!'

'What's up now?' asked Dresley, leaning over the windowsill.

'I think something's wrong with my eyes tonight,' his friend grunted. 'First I see lights winking in turrets – now I see enormous bubbles – look up there!'

Dresley looked. Already stinging slightly from his 'ignorance' of the disposition of Mr. Harrison's observatory, he had again missed the sight of whatever it was that Gregory had seen now. He peered from the window searching the skies.

'I don't – yes, I *do*!' he gasped suddenly.

They watched, silently. From north or north-west there drifted this strange form, seemingly the size of a football, and almost transparent. Gregory would not have seen it had he not been taking a final glance at the lofty turret: it was then that the 'bubble' had floated into his field of vision, drifting from the stark silhouette of the battlements and rooftops into the clear expanse of the sky.

'It's rising, slowly!' said Dresley, climbing on to the windowsill and gazing upwards.

'Look out, you'll fall through my kite, you ass!'

Dres teetered precariously and stopped gazing upwards in order to regain his balance. Then they stared skywards again; but now, only a few minutes after its first appearance, the bubble was fading, moment by moment, into invisibility.

'It's – vanished!'

Gregory nodded.

'Made of something transparent, I'd say.'

'Made of?'

'Of course. What d'you imagine it is, then?'

'I dunno. It looked like a sort of gigantic bit of flying frog's spawn to me.'

'Flying frog's spawn . . .' muttered Gregory. 'Sure it wasn't a suet pudding, driven by elastic?' He lifted his kite again. 'Come on, take this inside, and we'll see if we can find the way to that turret!'

Dresley fell off the windowsill with a cautious thud, and took the kite inside, taking care not to scrape the delicate flaps, rigging, ailerons and vanes against the edges of the window.

They made their way across West Hall and up the wide staircase. Gregory's whisper came :.

'I'm leaving this in the Study – hang on for me!'

A couple of minutes later he joined Dresley again at the head of the stairs.

'Now – d'you know anything about the geography of this place?'

Dresley tried to remember his north from his south, now they were inside the building.

'If we go up past the Library, and round by the Prefects' Gallery, we can try the stairs to the attics,' he suggested.

'Good egg. Come on. . . .'

They reached the Library, walking quickly in their rubber-soled shoes. From the long, circular Prefects' Gallery they looked down for a moment into the well of the West wing, where a few pale shafts of moonlight were slanting through the tall windows.

'Here are the stairs,' Dresley murmured, feeling

his way more cautiously, for it was almost pitchy dark.

They went up the stairs, making little sound over the heavy stone. There were no floorboards or wooden stairs here to creak and announce their presence. It made their journey easier, and quieter.

'Which way now?' breathed Gregory, when they reached a fourth flight of stairs in the gloom.

'My guess won't be any better than yours. If we—' He broke off.

'What now?'

'There's a door just here. I can feel it. You know something, Greggy?'

'Well?'

'This is a turret door.'

'We're not high enough!'

'We're near the top of the building, I'll tell you that much. These turrets have a door opening directly into them, below which is a flight of stairs, then another door. Like *this* one.'

Gregory frowned in the darkness.

'Wish we had a giddy lamp up here.'

'Yes, or a searchlight and a brass band,' breathed Dres Burgess. 'After all, we've got to let the cove know we're after him, haven't we?'

'All right,' Gregory agreed softly, 'in we go, then.'

'The door may be bolted on the—' Again he broke off. The door was not bolted. The handle turned easily, and the hinges, ancient and massive though they were, gave no hint of sound.

'Been oiled,' whispered Dresley.

A cooler passage of air now moved against their

faces, as if a window somewhere were open to the night. There was also a faint odour of wax.

'Candle. Smell it?' Gregory said softly.

Dresley Burgess nodded, then realized that a nod was just as useless as a wink in the darkness.

'Yes,' he breathed. A moment later they stopped. They had reached the second door; but it was half open. Through the gap between the timber and the post they glimpsed the gleam of stars. There was no sound here. Nor any candle-light.

Gregory felt a nudge on his shoulder-blade. Taking it as a signal for attack, he went forward, pushing open the heavy door with his left shoulder, prepared to defend himself against any unknown enemy. Dresley was beside him with a rush.

The turret was small, and dimly lighted by the stars. It had no furnishings, no rug or drapery by the narrow windows. It contained nothing except a single white candle, stuck into the neck of a bottle. The smell of the candle was now strong and pungent in their nostrils, and when Gregory put a hand out and felt the wick, he felt the soft heat of the wax immediately below. The flame had been burning only seconds ago.

11

THE CLUE IN THE CYCLE-SHED

BOB MAYFIELD lifted his stentorian voice.

'Show a leg there!'

Gregory dozed, blissfully.

'Up, Guards, and at 'em!'

Dresley Burgess stirred in his bed.

'Fire!' shouted Bob. 'Murder! Help! All hands on deck!'

Stevens and Burgess groaned, almost in unison, as the ear-shattering roar persisted, wrecking their last remaining dreams.

'Come on, you men!' chuckled Jim Raymond, pulling on his trousers. 'You've got about fifteen minutes!'

'Fifteen minutes,' murmured Greg Stevens, peering sleepily from his bed. 'Can we suffocate Mayfield in fifteen minutes, Dres?'

'Take longer than that,' grunted Burgess.

'Then there's only one alternative,' Gregory grumbled, crawling out of his bedclothes.

'And that's to get up,' nodded Dresley, following his lead reluctantly.

Jim looked at his weary friends.

'Where did you chaps get to last night?' he asked curiously. 'You don't seem to have had much sleep.'

'Flying kites,' murmured Dresley.

'Chasing bubbles,' grunted Gregory.

'And finding candles,' nodded Dresley.

While Jim Raymond eyed them doubtfully, wondering whether they were still wrapped in their dreams, they tottered out of the dormer, bathwards. Jim shrugged. His two friends had returned from their nocturnal errand, whatever it was; and so had the South American, del Pino. Jim had seen him within a few moments of waking. On his way down to breakfast, he paused by the new kid's bed.

'Glad you're back in time for morning roll-call,' he said quietly.

Del Pino knotted his tie carefully.

'Why should I not be?' he asked, calmly enough.

'You cut dormer-roll last night. I thought you might do the same thing this morning, that's all.'

'I must apologize. I was too busy to attend.'

Jim looked at him squarely. 'By your tone, del Pino, I imagine you intend doing the same thing again. Is that right?'

'The same thing?'

'Yes. Cutting roll-call.'

'Perhaps. Why?'

Jim kept his control as well as he could in the face of this deliberate provocation.

'Because the next time you do it I shall send a report in to Mr. Jackersby. Not because I like reporting chaps but because you're wasting my time. I've done my best to make you see reason; in future I'll leave it to Jacko. Try not to forget.'

Jim walked out of Long Dormer, fuming a little.

There was no opportunity of talking to his friends about the night's events before the first class, and then came a chance utterly unexpected. The first subject was Geology: and rumour had it that Mr. Harrison had been making observations from his turret during the night and had, as a result, overslept this morning. The class certainly had to wait some fifteen minutes for him, and this period of freedom gave the Quartet an opportunity of comparing notes.

'What d'you mean, Greggy, you were "kite-flying but didn't"?' asked Jim Raymond, his geological text-book open in front of him at the wrong place.

'We went to fly the Special Super-Hyper-Kite,' answered Dresley for him, 'but got interrupted.' And between them they told Jim and Bob Mayfield how they had seen the light in the turret, had, a moment later, seen the strange 'bubble' in the sky, and had discovered the still-warm candle in the lofty chamber above the West wing of the School buildings.

Jim Raymond looked at Gregory.

'You're the expert on aeronautics, Greg. What would you say the thing really was?'

Gregory Stevens sat back in his desk, tapping the lid reflectively with his ruler.

'Some type of balloon, I'd say. Made of transparent material to keep it as invisible as possible. But why it shouldn't be seen, I can't think.'

'Could it have been a Met-balloon, from the Research Station in Harleyfield?' queried Jim.

'Met-balloons aren't transparent,' said Gregory. 'And it was flying the other way in any case. It was going down-wind from the direction of the School.'

'And it's my guess,' nodded Dresley Burgess, 'that whoever was in that turret with a lighted candle was the cove who released the giddy thing.'

'Del Pino!' said Bob Mayfield.

Jim shrugged.

'Possibly, but not necessarily,' he said. 'He was out of the dormer last night, but so were Dres and Gregory.'

'It might have been a prefect or a beak,' suggested Bob.

'Old Harry!' said Dresley, his face clearing suddenly. 'He might be using that turret as well as the one where he stables his telescope!'

They thought over the suggestion; then Jim shook his head.

'Something tells me it's murky work. Old Harry is an amateur astronomer, and chaps like that don't go about flying invisible bubbles. The whole scheme seems fishy to me.'

'We could ask Harrison, gently,' suggested Gregory.

'We could,' nodded Jim slowly. 'And we could also ask del Pino.'

'What did the kid say when you asked him why he cut roll?' Bob wanted to know.

'He said he apologized, but was too busy.'

'Of all the howling cheek!'

Jim nodded briefly.

'The next time he plays the devil I shall just report him to Jacko and wash my hands of him. I don't mind when a chap tries to co-operate, but—'

'I think he's had enough rope,' agreed Bob. 'D'you think a bang on the proboscis might change his mind for him?'

'I don't like that way of tackling the problem.'

'No, but I'd enjoy it,' grinned Bob belligerently.

'Maybe. Anyhow, I'll ask Harrison if he knows anything of a balloon; if he doesn't, I'll ask del Pino.'

'Not that you'll get a word out of him if—' began Dresley, when the warning came:

'*Ppsstt* – beak!'

'*Cave,* you men!'

There was a shuffling of feet, a rustling of paper as many books were opened in a hurry; and the murmur of voices died away, a moment before the footsteps of Mr. Harrison – heard by some sharp ear – paused outside the door.

'Good morning, boys!'

He bustled in, panting a little and with his gown hastily donned, and went straight to his desk on the low rostrum.

'I am late, I fear. However, I am glad there was no uproar in my absence. Kindly turn to page sixty-three in your *Geological Elements and Formations*.'

The class began. But its beginning was unusual on this occasion.

'Before we begin, I should like to ask if there is any boy here who possesses a large balloon.'

The silence was a startled one. To most of the

chaps the word 'balloon' conjured the vision of a large pink, blue or green object usually to be seen in surroundings decorated with holly, mistletoe and paper-chains. But in summer-time, surely no member of the Fourth would possess such a childish toy!

'A large balloon,' added Mr. Harrison, as Jim Raymond exchanged a glance with his three friends, 'constructed of some transparent material.' He looked at his pupils over his desk.

Jim was observing the reactions of a boy sitting a few yards away from him – del Pino's. But the new kid appeared to be as surprised and as puzzled by this extraordinary question as did the other chaps.

'Very well,' nodded "Old Harry", and sat down, drawing his gown around his legs. 'It so happened that last night, when I was observing the planet Mars . . . Mayfield, the diameter of Mars?'

'Er – er – four thousand two hundred miles, sir!'

'Good. As I was observing that planet with whose dimensions our friend Mayfield is so creditably familiar, I also observed a balloon, floating above the School buildings. No one here, however, knows anything of it. We shall therefore pass on to our more proper subject.'

It was at 'break' when Jim Raymond had an opportunity of asking del Pino the same question that he had intended to ask Mr. Harrison, before that gentleman had broached the subject himself. As the Quartet strolled along the edge of the Quadrangle, near where the avenue of beeches cast their dappling shade, they saw the South American under the roof of the long cycle-stand adjoining the Gymnasium.

'There's our little night-bird,' murmured Bob Mayfield, 'working on his speed-iron.'

They drifted across. Several chaps were oiling, cleaning or tinkering with their bicycles. Del Pino was just pumping his front tyre, and on the ground was his puncture outfit.

'Got pins and needles in the tubes?' asked Dresley, as the Company of Four halted, watching with mild interest.

'Yes, but it's fixed now,' said del Pino, feeling the tyre for hardness. He disconnected the pump.

'By the way,' said Jim Raymond, 'you didn't happen to see anything of that flying bubble last night, did you?'

Del Pino snapped the connexion into the handle of the pump with a deft movement.

'Flying bubble?' he asked, frowning.

'The balloon,' nodded Jim. Bob, Dres and Gregory watched, saying nothing.

'Why should I have, Raymond?'

'Simply because you were out of the dormer. I thought you might have glimpsed the thing on your travels.'

'What do you mean by "travels"?'

'It's merely an expression meaning—'

'I was travelling nowhere,' cut in the new boy curtly, 'and I saw nothing of any flying bubble. Had I done so I should have replied to Mr. Harrison's question in form this morning.'

Jim shrugged, turning away.

'I just asked, del Pino. Forget it.'

They heard the South American's retort as they strolled off towards the avenue of beeches.

'I shall forget it. And I should advise you to do the same, if you prefer not to get hurt.'

Jim half turned in surprise, then thought better of an argument. Something told him that it would be more useful to let the matter lie than to probe it too deeply just now.

'Why didn't you pin his ears to the bike-shed wall?' asked Bob Mayfield, with a thunderous brow.

'I'd rather get to the truth by other means,' replied Jim tersely. 'I've already got a clue, though it may want some working out.'

'Clue?' asked Dresley, as they moved under the trees.

'Yes. He didn't like the way I said "travelling" – did you notice?'

'It caught him on the wrong foot,' nodded Gregory Stevens.

Jim spoke quietly. 'And did you notice anything else? His tyres?'

'He'd been mendin' punctures,' nodded Bob Mayfield.

'That was bright of you,' grunted Jim, 'considering the puncture-set was littering the ground. But there was something else. They were covered in chalk.'

'Chalk?'

'Precisely. He'd been riding over chalky ground – possibly during last night. And where's the nearest chalky ground from here?'

'There's none that I've seen,' frowned Gregory.

'You mean he's been ridin' over Harleyfield Downs?' exclaimed Bob Mayfield.

Dresley looked at Jim quickly.

'But that's five miles from here!' he said.

Jim nodded. 'Not far, on a bike. And where does Harleyfield lie from here – north?'

'Due south,' corrected Gregory, puzzled.

'Exactly. Where did you say that flying bubble was heading?'

'South!' exclaimed Dresley. 'Towards the Downs! But I still don't see—'

'Nor do I, Dres,' cut in Jim Raymond, 'but there might be something that connects everything up. Let me work on it for a bit and if I can think of any answer I'll let you know.'

12

THE SECRET CIPHER

PODGER PEPYS held his breath.

Slowly the footsteps loudened, reached the door, then faded, as slowly, down the passage. Podger Pepys released his breath. He began his careful search anew.

The facts at the master-sleuth's command were simply these: that new kid, del Pino, had displayed an extraordinary interest in this Study since he arrived at Monks' Court. He carried a knife. He flitted from Long Dormer by night. And now he had forsaken Study Six for some unknown clime. On top of which little edifice of curious facts was the latest topic of conversation in the School: the Flying Bubble.

So Podger Pepys was investigating the Case of del Pino. And there was a chance of his inquiries merging with another: the Case of the Flying Bubble. There might be some connexion between the two. Had the South American been building an invisible balloon in this very room, on Sunday afternoon, and at night – the night Podger followed him from Long

Dormer? Had he taken it away to that turret, for more secrecy, to complete the building of it prior to its flight last night? Why build a balloon? Why make it almost invisible? Why carry a knife? If someone else was making the secret bubble, was del Pino in some sort of opposition to him and his plans?

'Sly beast!' murmured the super-sleuth. There seemed to be nowhere else to search. What he was searching for he did not know. A clue of some sort, of course – a bomb that would tick ominously when he discovered its malevolent shape; or a machine-gun, loaded and still warm; or perhaps . . .

Podger stared. At this moment his alert, observant eyes (keener than any hawk's) were resting upon a small pile of text-books that del Pino had thrown on to the table before going down to tea. There was a red book (Locking's *French Verse*), there was a blue book (Allen and White – *Physical Elements*), there was a brown book (*Intermediary Trigonometry, Grade II*), and there was a black book.

Podger approached the black book on the table and picked it from between the red and the blue ones. There was no indented title upon the soft leather cover, nor the name of its author, nor the imprint of its publisher. It was a perfectly plain black cover.

Sexton Pepys opened it.

Had there been footsteps in the passage at this moment he would not have heeded them; he was too enwrapped in what he read – or, more accurately, what he could *not* read. For the writing, which was in careful, orderly longhand, was indecipherable. It was, in fact, in cipher.

The brain of Podger Pepys, even when geared to the high-speed activities of Sherlock Blake, was not noted for its nimbleness. But he realized two things at once, as he stood peering at the book of code-writing. One was that he could not make away with this book without arousing del Pino's suspicions of his Study-mate; and two – he must take a copy of as much of the writing as was possible before the author came on the scene.

With an unhesitating movement, Sexton Pepys whipped out a pen and began taking a copy of the cipher-writing on a leaf of one of his own exercise-books. The first line occupied him less than sixty seconds:

Ibsmfzgjfme Sftfbsdi Tubujpo fohbhfe po bupnjd fyqfsjnfout.

The next line, written a little more hurriedly by del Pino, took longer, and it was towards the end of it that Podger Blake heard the first faint footfalls of chaps returning from tea. He hurried with his task and managed to copy:

Xjmm buufnqu qipuphsbqit cz ojhiu . . .

And now there was the definite danger of the South American's coming straight into Study Six. He would not even pause to knock, since it was his own room and Pepys's. Podger made an anxious blob with the pen, copied one more word:

vtjoh . . .

and closed the book with a snap, slipping it between the others and shutting his own exercise-book. The pen was in his pocket a second later, and not a second too soon, for the door opened suddenly and del Pino entered.

'Hello, Pepys,' said del Pino, casting him a puzzled look. 'What's the matter?' He picked up the pile of books, put them under his arm, and turned to the door.

'N-nothing, old ch-chap! I was just – I mean I'm s-so glad t-to see you! Why don't you s-sit down and m-make yourself at home?'

Del Pino paused only for a moment to stare in slight bewilderment at the confused Podge, then he shrugged and left the Study. The door closed.

Podger gulped. But at least he had made progress – brilliant progress! He had found the cipher-book and had even copied the first two lines of its writing. What might they not reveal, once deciphered?

Podger Pepys lost his fright, clutched his exercise-book to his ample bosom, and left the Study, going down to the playing-fields where many of the members of Winston were walking in the late-afternoon sunshine, practising at the nets and making up impromptu cricket matches. 'Prep' would be left until later on these warm summer evenings.

Lowering his bulk gently to the grass, Sexton

Pepys took the exercise-book, opened it, and produced his pen. He had not read upwards of a hundred detective novels for nothing.

The pen moved in the hand of Podger Pepys. Trying the simplest cipher he knew – where a word is written backwards and given a prefix-letter and a suffix-letter to mislead the curious reader – he copied the first word, '*Ibsmfzgjfme*', then crossed off the first and last letter, and wrote the word backwards. Had the word had been 'cat', it would have been coded as 'otacs', and by removing the end letters and reading backwards the solution would have been simple enough. But with the same test, Podger was left with '*Mfjgzfmsb*' – which meant nothing at all to him.

'Sly scoundrel,' he murmured, and tried another test. Taking 'a' as 'z', 'b' as 'y', 'c' as 'x', and so on, by which cipher the word 'cat' would code as 'xzg', he wrote the first word down in its new form. The result was '*Ryhnuatqunv*'.

'Cunning beast!' grunted the disgruntled Podge, no nearer the solution. He tried another test, and produced a word quite unrecognizable. Another, and was faced with a word utterly unintelligible. Another, and derived a word without any possible meaning.

'Crafty rascal!' he declared, blinking indignantly at his collection of gibberish. He had now run out of ciphers. That there were a thousand more he was aware, but he did not know how they worked.

Putting his pen away into his pocket, and thereby adding it to a collection of string, toffees, a scone left over from tea, a penknife and a length of chalk, he closed the exercise-book and lay back, resting his head on his plump and pillowing hands. His eyes closed. Sherlock Pepys, wearied of his activities in the interests of law, order and justice, slept.

He slept soundly: that is to say deeply and noisily. He slept until the shadows were long, reaching across the sun-warm grass from the beeches to the cricket pavilion. And when he awoke there was crick in his neck, and he was stiff. Most of the fellows seemed to have gone in to do their 'prep'.

Podger remembered, in an instant, the task that had been absorbing his keen, astute intelligence before he had dozed into oblivion. He would have one more try, now that his master-brain had been rested and refreshed by the tonic of slumber, before he went up to Study Six. He produced his pen from his pocket, popped a toffee into his capacious mouth, and put his hand out for the exercise-book.

But it was gone.

13

ONE VITAL WORD

Jim Raymond hitched himself on to his favourite perch, the wide windowsill of Study Four, and folded his arms. In the armchair sprawled Dresley Burgess, his long legs stretched out in front of him. Bob Mayfield was binding the blade of his cricket-bat with tape and Gregory Stevens was making a modification to his super-kite on the table.

'Now we'll begin at the beginning,' said Jim Raymond.

Podger Pepys was not the only fellow in the Fourth Form of Winston House who was investigating 'The Case of del Pino', together with 'The Case of the Flying Bubble'. Jim Raymond, Head Boy of the Form and acknowledged leader of the Company of Four, had been asked personally by Mr. Jackersby, Housemaster of Winston, to inquire into strange activities of the new boy, del Pino.

'Point one,' said Jim, 'is that, from his first appearance here, del Pino stuck to his Study like a cockle to a rock. He was in there on Sunday afternoon and during the night – apart from normal periods.'

'Point two,' said Dres Burgess from the depths of his armchair, 'is that our fat friend Bulldozer Pepys said the new kid threatened him with a knife.'

'We might take that statement with a pinch of salt,' cut in Gregory, fixing a balsa-wood cross-member to his kite. 'You know old Podge when he lets himself go – it was probably a small nail file.'

'Be that as it may,' shrugged Jim Raymond; 'point three is that suddenly del Pino has deserted Study Six. He's never seen there, except to collect his text-books or something like that.'

'Point four, then,' said Gregory, 'is that he might have moved from the Study to that turret where Dresley and I found the candle.'

'That could be,' nodded Jim. 'A fifth point is the business of the Flying Bubble. Did del Pino make it and fly it last night? Why?'

'And if he did,' put in Bob Mayfield, 'where did he go on his mechanical horse? To follow the bubble?'

'Point six,' nodded Jim, 'the bubble was drifting south, towards Harleyfield Downs; and there was chalk on del Pino's tyres, possibly from the Downs.'

They were silent for a while. Their list of facts had come to an end; yet there appeared to be no common factor, unless it was Harleyfield.

'What say we take it in turns to keep watch on the chap at night?' suggested Dresley.

'He's too fly.' Jim shook his head. 'It isn't easy to follow a chap in dead silence and pitch darkness, especially through this old building where every timber creaks.'

Again there fell silence. Ideas seemed to be sticking.

'Suppose we . . .' Bob Mayfield began, and broke off. A pair of exceptionally noisy feet had stopped outside the door of the Study, and now an exceptionally noisy knock made itself more than heard upon the panels.

'I've got a code!' announced the portly Pepys, closing the door with an excited bang. He blinked vigorously at the Company of Four.

'Poor old Podge,' said Dres Burgess; 'got a code, have you? Why dode you drig sub code-cure, thed?'

'Don't trifle, Burgess,' said Pepys severely. 'This is important. Urgent! Life or death, in – in fact.'

'Then it isn't a code you've got,' said Gregory, 'it's triple pneumonia. Better cut and see Matron, old bean.'

'That's no good,' grinned Bob Mayfield, 'he'll only tell her atishoo of lies.'

'Of course if you fellows aren't interested,' snorted the portly and disappointed purveyor of important information, 'I don't really think I should stay.'

'Oh, what a shame!' cried Bob Mayfield. 'I was saying only a moment ago, "I *do* wish old Podge would come and see us!"'

'Were you really, Mayfield?'

'I was, dear Podge. I was trying to convince my friend Burgess that a human being can consume ten hundredweight of food per day and still live. You were the best example I could think of.'

'Well, really, Mayfield! I shall certainly go!' He

turned for the door with a fat and indignant flourish. 'If you think I'm going to say a word to you beasts about del Pino's little secrets, you're mistaken, I assure you!'

He opened the door. As he was about to walk out he felt a hand grip the back of his blazer, another the seat of his trousers – and instead of walking through the doorway in a forward direction he found himself propelled backwards with his feet off the ground. It was really most extraordinary.

'*Hooops!* Leave me alone!'

'Would you kindly repeat that, Podger?'

'I said *"Hooops!* Leave me alone!"' scowled Pepys.

'No, I mean the bit about del Pino,' said Jim gently.

Podger regarded the leader of the Quartet.

'Since you seem prepared to listen, Raymond, I might be prepared to tell you.' But his eyes roamed the Study before he spoke again. Since tea he had slept on the grass where there was now dew rising. He was therefore hungry again. 'I'm not sure I can remember *all* of it,' he added. 'It isn't easy when I'm famished, you know – I just can't seem to concentrate, somehow.'

'Come on, Podgy,' Jim said quietly. 'You came here to tell us something. What was it?'

'I think if I could just have something to stop my feeling so faint,' said Pepys weakly, brushing a feeble hand across his brow, 'I might—'

'Give you three seconds,' said Bob Mayfield.

'One . . .' nodded Jim.

'Two . . .' intoned Gregory.

'Three . . .' added Dresley – but Podger Pepys lifted an uneasy hand.

'I'm sure there's no need for crude threats,' he said nervously. 'I came here to offer my assistance in the case of del Pino. While you men have been puzzling over it I have naturally been making exhaustive inquiries and conducting exorbitant investigations into the matter.'

'Or something like that,' murmured Gregory.

'Please be quiet, Stevens. Your interruptions will tend to confuse the superficialities.'

'Go on, Podger,' invited Jim Raymond.

'Well, it was like this. I was searching del Pino's locker in Study Six, and . . . I mean I was standing there thinking about how peculiar the chap was, when an idea came to me. I said to myself, "I wonder if that scoundrel del Pino has got a book with code-writing in it?" '

'I hope you left the locker just as you found it,' murmured Bob Mayfield with a grin.

'I never touched the locker! It was the desk I searched most thoroughly! I – I mean I never searched anything! I suppose you think I'm the sort of fellow who goes prying into a Study-mate's private possessions?'

'I do,' nodded Jim. 'Proceed, Peepers, if you please.'

'Well, really, Raymond!'

'Yes, truly, Podger,' nodded Jim. 'Where did you find this book of code?'

'On the table, among his text-books!'

'Have you got it with you?' asked Gregory, losing interest for a moment in his kite.

'No. I hardly go about stealing fellows' books, Stevens!'

'Did you take a copy?' asked Dresley.

'I certainly did,' nodded Pepys, impressed with his own astuteness. 'Some of it, anyway. That fool del Pino came barging in and interrupted me.'

'Where's the copy, Podge?' asked Jim Raymond.

'I had it on a page of an exercise-book of my own, and I took it down to the playing-fields to decipher the writing, but while I was sitting there del Pino stole up behind me, clapped a pad of methylated spirits over my face, and ran off with the book, leaving me drugged and helpless! Of course I staggered to my feet and—'

'Hold on, Podger!' cut in Jim. 'You mean you dozed off, I suppose?'

'Haven't I just said that? I dozed off, exactly, and while I slept del Pino stole up behind me, raised a blackjack, and brought it down with all his weight on top of—'

'When you woke up from this amazing dream,' corrected Jim, 'you found the book had been taken away. Is that about it?'

'So it was you, was it?' hooted Podge energetically. 'Look here, Raymond, if you stole my book, I'll—'

'Don't be crass, you ass! Did you actually see del Pino take it?'

'If I had, I'd have tackled him low and brought him crashing to the ground, wouldn't I?'

'No.' Jim slipped from the windowsill and paced up and down a little, frowning. 'So you found a book of code, made a copy of some of it, went to sleep in the playing-fields, and woke up to find the exercise-book missing. That right?'

'Of course. Naturally I put up a fierce struggle, but—'

'Where is the book you copied from, Podgy?' asked Jim, stopping and looking down at his portly visitor.

'That beast del Pino came for it, and nearly caught me with it. He took it away, with the others.'

Gregory Stevens spread out his hands.

'The position, then, is precisely as it was before.'

'Except,' said Dresley, 'that we know del Pino has a book written in cipher of some sort.'

'Of course,' Bob put in, 'it might be about any-thing – something innocent, I mean. Plenty of chaps keep a private diary in Greek or some kind of code.'

Podger Pepys glared up at his guests.

'If you fellows will allow me to speak,' he said warmly, 'I shall continue.'

'Sorry, Podger,' said Jim, 'we thought that was all you had to tell.'

'My information is scarcely as trivial as that, Raymond. I lost the exercise-book, and I'm perfectly sure that del Pino walked past where I was – er – resting, and pinched it. But I can write out the first word of the code from memory.'

'You can?'

'Give him a pencil, someone!'

Podger sat enthroned, filled with personal gratification, while Jim Raymond snapped a pen from the pocket of his blazer and passed it to him.

'Here's some paper, Podgy,' said Gregory, passing him a sheet of foolscap.

'Thank you, my dear Stevens. Now, if you'll allow me to concentrate a moment . . .'

'There you are,' he said triumphantly.

Jim Raymond looked over his shoulder. Bob Mayfield leaned forward, gazing at the word. Gregory Stevens and Dresley Burgess nudged each other vigorously as they packed themselves into the circle of audience. The little word stared up at them from the sheet of paper:

Ibsmfzgjfme.

'Are you sure that's correct?' asked Jim, frowning over it.

Podger blinked.

'I never make mistakes, my dear fellow.'

They looked again at the curious word. And for the next half an hour there was silence in Study Four, except for an occasional suggestion from one or the other of the Quartet.

Podger Pepys was munching at a pineapple in the corner, having been offered it by Bob Mayfield as a stop-gap between tea and supper. The fat detective had certainly discovered a clue; and if it had almost been snatched from his grasp soon afterwards, at least he had salvaged one single word of the coded writing. Even that might give them a new lead in 'The Case of del Pino'.

'It isn't spelt backwards with a prefix-letter and a suffix-letter,' said Jim Raymond at last.

'And it isn't the reverse-alphabet key,' grunted Gregory Stevens.

'Nor is it written backwards in any foreign language that we're familiar with,' added Dresley Burgess.

'There's one method we haven't tried,' murmured Jim, 'but that's going to take a long time.'

'What is it, Chief?'

'There are twenty-six variations,' he told them. 'And it might be any one of them.'

Gregory's face cleared suddenly.

'You mean 'a' equals 'z', 'b' equals 'y' – and so on?'

'No, we've tried that – that's the reverse-alphabet key. I mean this one: 'a' equals 'b', 'b' equals 'c', 'c' equals 'd' and so on.'

Bob Mayfield scratched his head.

'I don't twig,' he said, 'but let's try it.'

Quickly Jim Raymond wrote the word anew, putting in the place of each original letter the letter that preceded it in the alphabet. 'I' became 'h', 'b' became 'a', 's' became 'r' – until, when he was half-way through the word, Gregory Stevens caught his breath.

'That's the key, Jim! It's the first of the twenty-six variations!'

'Look,' said Bob triumphantly, 'it's making sense!'

Jim nodded, continuing swiftly with the task that was, so suddenly, simplicity itself. 'Ibs' had become 'Har', 'mfz' was now 'ley' – and in another moment the word was before them on the sheet of foolscap.

The name was 'Harleyfield'.

'Harleyfield Downs!' cried Bob Mayfield.

'Where the chalk on those tyres came from!' added Dresley.

'And in the direction of which that Flying Bubble was making!' breathed Jim Raymond. 'Podger, you've got something here!'

VIGIL IN THE STARLIGHT

FOR three days and three nights there came no development in what was now called by the Quartet 'The Case of del Pino's Bubble'. This title had been decided upon because now that Podger Pepys had snatched the word 'Harleyfield' from the South American's coded notebook, they were certain that it provided the link they had been seeking – the link between del Pino's activities in Study Six and later in some place unknown by any.

But for three days and three nights del Pino, the obstinate, arrogant South American new-boy, offered no single hint of trouble. He attended every roll-call. He was never seen in his Study at any period when the Studies were out of bounds. He was never absent from the dormitory – as far as any of the other fellows were able to discover.

'I'll tell you why he's become such a paragon of excellence,' Gregory Stevens told his friends confidently.

'Well?' Jim asked him interestedly.

'It's the wind.'

They stared at the aeronautical expert.

'The wind?' echoed Bob Mayfield. 'You mean it affects his brain, like the giddy stars and planets?'

'I'd say something's affecting yours,' grunted Gregory, 'because I don't mean anything so absurdly crass. No, it's just that the wind has been set due south for the past three nights.'

'Tell us more, Greggy,' invited Dres Burgess.

'Well, every night, before dormer roll-call, I nip down to the Quad to test the wind-direction—'

'What on earth for?' cut in Jim Raymond.

'To see if it's in the right direction for testing my kite – north or north-west. Otherwise it'll fly into the building. Anyway, the wind's been from the south for the past three nights.'

'Which means del Pino can't fly his balloon either!' said Bob Mayfield, seeing the light.

'Exactly – because it has to fly over towards Harley-field Downs,' nodded Gregory. 'They're south of here, and he can't fly the thing straight into the wind.'

Jim Raymond pursed his lips.

'So until the wind changes,' he said slowly, 'he's lying low. And that's why no one's seen the Flying Bubble again at night!'

'Another reason for us to connect the two of them – del Pino and the Bubble!' said Dresley Burgess.

Jim Raymond walked over to the door of the Study where they were talking, opened it, looked out into the passage, closed it, and came back.

'Listen, you men,' he said quietly. 'I've an idea.

118

If it comes off we can nab del Pino at his little game, and solve the mystery of the Bubble at the same time.'

Bob Mayfield glanced at his chief seriously.

'Shoot,' he said briefly.

Wasting no time and no words, Jim Raymond shot his plan, detailing it for his three friends as they listened without interruption.

. . . . .

For those three days and those three nights nothing had occurred that might prove to be a development in 'The Case of del Pino's Bubble', but on the fourth night something did.

It began by the changing of the wind.

At about nine o'clock, when most of the Fourth Formers were in their Studies or the Junior Common Room of Winston House, Gregory Stevens went down through the West Hall, out of the main doors, and into the Quadrangle.

Walking clear of the buildings that would shield any wind from the north, north-west or north-east, Gregory stood motionless, and in a moment felt the gentle movement of a breeze that drifted past the tumbled buildings and carried softly across the playing-fields to South Meadow and beyond, among the trees of Banner Wood. What wind there was came from the north, down from the Surrey hills.

'Well?' asked Jim Raymond when Gregory returned to the Study.

'North,' he said briefly.

'Strong?' asked Bob Mayfield.

'No, just a breeze – but enough to lift my kite, if I took it down there.'

Dresley looked at him. 'And enough to drift that Bubble, Greggy?'

'Certainly. It hasn't got to be lifted, because it's my guess it's filled with some sort of lighter-than-air gas. Once airborne, the slightest breeze will carry it slowly for as long as the breeze lasts.'

Jim looked at his three comrades.

'Right,' he said. 'Are you chaps game?'

Bob Mayfield looked at his wrist-watch.

'It's worth a try,' he said. 'If Greggy thinks del Pino's been waiting for the wind to change, tonight's the night.'

'Hold on for a moment,' Jim told them, and left the Study. Going down the corridor, he tapped at the door of Study Six.

'G-go away!' came a squeak from inside. 'I mean I'm n-not here!' And there was a dull thud.

Jim Raymond chuckled and opened the door.

'You did say "come in", didn't you?' he asked, peering in.

'Oh, it's you, Raymond! Th-thank goodness! I thought it was that rotter del Pino!'

Jim closed the door, puzzled. It was clear by the disposition of the chair in the corner that Podger had been inspecting the contents of the tall cupboard. And judging by Podger's relief, it was del Pino's cupboard.

'I'm still looking for my exercise-book,' volunteered the plump sleuth. 'But there's not a sniff of it yet.'

'I doubt if you'll find that again, Podge. He'll have burned it, most likely. I came to ask if you'd seen anything of him this evening.'

'Not a wink. Not since tea. Have you found any clues?'

'No, but we're going to look for some tonight. If we're missed from the dormer, do your best to cover up for us, will you, Podger?'

'Leave it to me, my dear Raymond. Just leave the control in my capable hands. And if you make any discovery, let me know the details and I'll give you the solution.'

Jim gave a grin and opened the door.

'I forgot you were in charge of this case, old bean,' he said respectfully.

'It's obviously a case for a really clever mind to solve, Raymond, and I'm afraid I shall have to spend a few more days on it yet. But I'm grateful for your assistance, all the same. It's much easier for me to pit my wits against the lawless when I have the services of such willing assistants.'

Jim closed the door on these last words, not wishing to hurt the fat detective's feelings by broadening his chuckle in his presence. He reached Study Four again.

'All right, you chaps. Del Pino hasn't been near his room all evening.'

'Which means,' replied Gregory Stevens, 'that he's been testing the wind as well as me.'

Jim Raymond nodded.

'You chaps carry on as planned, and I'll see you at roll-call. All right?'

Bob Mayfield, Gregory Stevens and Dresley Burgess left Study Four, strolling down the passage in the direction of West Hall. After which they were not seen until the Fourth Form forgathered in Long Dormer prior to bed. Jim Raymond, as soon as his friends had left the Study, strolled along the corridor in the opposite direction, and for the next ten or fifteen minutes spoke to several fellows – just in passing – to learn from them – quite casually – that they had seen nothing of del Pino all this evening since tea.

It was not long before the Quartet's suspicions were confirmed. The wind had changed; nothing had been seen of the South American all the evening; and now, when Jim Raymond called the roll, there were two absentees. One, Blairman by name, was in the Sanatorium with hay fever, the other, del Pino, was – where?

Bob, Dresley and Gregory answered their names with the others and, with the others, they turned into Long Dormer and appeared to prepare for bed. But some ten minutes after Mr. Jackersby had come along to put the lights out they slipped from the bedclothes and donned their gym shoes quietly.

.   .   .   .   .

'Over this way,' grunted Bob Mayfield. He was the first to speak a word since they had clambered through the window in West Hall. The others followed his direction, and within a few minutes found themselves in a small cluster of bushes at the wide end of South Meadow.

The starlight gleamed now upon metal. Bob, Gregory and Dresley had done their job well. Their four bicycles had been wheeled quietly from the cycle-sheds in the Quadrangle, lifted over the wall, and concealed in this knoll of bushes. When the three of them had answered their names at dormer-roll the task was already done.

Jim Raymond picked up his bicycle and straddled it. Greg Stevens tested his tyres with a quick pressure of his fingers, and leaned on his machine, hands in the pockets of his slacks. Dresley Burgess and Bob Mayfield mounted their saddles and leaned patiently with their arms across the handlebars.

The eyes of the Quartet were fixed unwaveringly upon the highest turrets of Monks' Court. In the warm silence, as though they were themselves a part of the starlit night, they waited, watching quietly.

15

HUNTERS AT MIDNIGHT

A MIST had risen, and now spread across South Meadow in grey, silent veils. The earth was losing the warmth of the day, and dew-spangled the grass, reflecting the light of the stars so that the meadows looked almost frosty on this summer's night.

'Call me at eight,' murmured Bob Mayfield, half-dozing across his handlebars.

Jim Raymond rubbed his eyes. Already he was struggling to keep awake, for the strain of watching the turrets of Monks' Court was telling. It was about eleven-thirty now, and normally the Company of Four would have been fast asleep.

Dresley Burgess played a quiet tattoo with his fingers on the crossbar of his machine, but his eyes never left the silhouetted frieze of turrets to the north.

'Look!'

'Where?' asked Bob, lifting his head and peering.

'The turret above the end of the West wing!'

As they stared, now fully roused, they saw the faint shape that was rising slowly towards the stars, breaking free from the stark outlines of the building.

'The balloon,' grunted Bob, 'has literally gone up!'

'Are you ready, you two?' asked Jim, watching the blurred, soaring shape that was now nearing from the School.

Dresley nodded.

'Ready, Greg?' he asked quickly.

'Contact,' Gregory responded, and ran his machine over the few yards of grass towards the roadway. Dresley followed, bumping his bicycle over the short, tufted turf. They mounted, waved a hand to Jim and Bob, and then turned their machines to the east, vanishing in a few moments behind the hedgerows.

The Bubble was almost overhead by now, and still rising. The plans of the Quartet, already worked out in detail, were simple enough. They expected the Bubble to follow its previous route: southwards over Banner Wood; they suspected that it would drift onwards across Harleyfield Downs, and they wanted to know why it was sent there, and what would happen to it once it had arrived above the chalky slopes. Therefore two of them were to follow the drifting mystery balloon for as far as it led them and for as long as it remained visible from the ground.

The other two, Jim and Bob, were to remain in the seclusion of the bushes, for they suspected that del Pino, after sending up the Bubble, would follow its direction on his bicycle – and gather more chalk from Harleyfield Downs on his tyres.

Already, within a few moments of the Bubble's

having been sighted above the turrets of Monks' Court, these simple plans were in operation. Dresley Burgess and Gregory Stevens were riding down the road towards Banner; Jim Raymond and Bob Mayfield were watching for a sign of another rider – del Pino – to appear from the direction of the School grounds.

Above the four of them (and was there now a fifth?) there drifted the Bubble, moving southwards at a speed of scarcely more than three or four miles per hour, for the breeze was slight. Now it was over South Meadow; in a moment it would near the darkling fringe of Banner Wood. There was no roadway, or even a path, leading due south from the School. To keep within sight of their flying quarry Dres and Gregory would have to ride fast down the road towards the village of Banner, turn right and cross the rickety old bridge that spanned the River Trayle and join the road beyond that ran south-west for about a mile; after which it turned south and wound, meandering, up the hill from whose brow the Downs could be seen in daylight.

Their tyres sang on the smooth roadway, and there was almost no other sound. Their machines had been oiled for this urgent journey; there was no excessive slack on the chains. To allow as little noise as possible in case they neared del Pino on the road, their mudguards, bells, pump-holders and brake systems had been tightened, so that there came not the slightest click or rattle as they sped down the starlit road.

In a moment they swerved into the narrow lane on their right hand, and accelerated for the bridge.

Its 'floor' was composed of narrow slats, and it was not more than four feet wide at any point.

'Keep going, Dres!' called Gregory, and slackened his speed a fraction. The first machine hit the slats and sped along them as Dresley strove to keep a straight course. Their lamps were not burning – again in case they neared del Pino anywhere along the route to the Downs – and although the starlight was almost as bright as a half-moon, it was not easy to ride at something approaching twenty miles an hour on to a four-foot-wide bridge over a swirling river.

Looking up, once, into the starry face of the heavens, Gregory tried to glimpse the Bubble; but either it had risen too high and had become, because of its semi-transparency, invisible, or it was too far westwards above Banner Wood to be seen from here. Whatever the reason, Gregory was forced to remove his gaze from the skies. He had taken his eyes from the path only for a moment, but now he had to swerve viciously to avoid the bole of an immense oak that stood, rearing as a sentinel, beside the route.

With the wood to their right they met the road to Harleyfield and turned westwards along it. The surface was smooth, the going was easier, for the road ran slightly downhill and, more important than either, they were now riding back to the airy course of the Bubble.

After half a mile Dresley slowed, glancing upwards as his companion called out:

'Look there, Dres!'

They slowed to a halt at the dusty edge of the road, nearby a knoll of larches. Above the tops of the trees, a little to the west, came that strange shape, drifting from the leafy crown of Banner Wood. It was almost as though a gigantic bead of water had been tossed up from the secret depths of a well bewitched, deep in the heart of the silent wood, and was now floating upon some airy, magic pathway above the trees.

'Come on, Dresley. The road goes west for another half-mile before we can get back to the southward course that Bubble's making.'

They stabbed the pedals again with their feet; the tyres bit into the dusty roadside. They rode west, away from the course of their quarry, before they could turn south up the winding hill and near its path again.

Across Banner Wood and the dewy expanse of South Meadow, Jim Raymond and Bob Mayfield were running their machines over the grass between the bushes and the Radford road. A moment ago they had seen what they had been hoping to see: the figure of someone riding a bicycle from the field adjoining the School First XI pitches.

Del Pino was following his Bubble.

As Jim leapt across the saddle, Bob grunted a warning:

'Fast as you can, Jim! He's making for South Meadow, at the lower end!'

'Come on, then!'

They built up their speed, saving their breath for the work. It was clear, already, that del Pino knew a more direct route to Harleyfield Downs than by the bridge across the Trayle that Dresley and Gregory had stormed a while ago. He had now vanished, but before long, when his pursuers found the gap in the fence, he was in sight again, riding the rough grass towards the wood. Then the trees claimed him, and he was lost among them.

Bob and Jim cleared the Meadow and found the pathway that del Pino must have taken. It ran, twisting and darting through the clustering timbers, straight to the heart of the wood.

Once or twice they glimpsed the gleam of metal ahead of them when there came a clearing in the trees, and once they halted, to strain their ears for a sound of the quarry. But none came. The path was smooth and del Pino was making no noise. Starting off again, his pursuers climbed from the depths of the wood and reached the first thinning of the timbers.

'See him?' panted Bob, halting on the smooth tarmac surface.

'Yes – there he goes!'

'After him then!' Jim grunted, and they jerked their machines to life again. Preparing for a half-mile ride down the smooth roadway, they were surprised for the second time on their journey. Within five hundred yards of Banner Wood del Pino slowed and stopped.

'Look out!' Bob panted. 'He's twigged us on his tail!'

Jim slid his machine to a halt and stared ahead of him.

'No,' he said quickly; 'he's leaving the road – look!'

The distant figure had glanced back once, and

then had lifted his cycle into the hedgerow. It seemed that he knew a second short cut to the Downs, apart from the path through Banner Wood.

'Give him a moment, Bob,' Jim warned.

They waited. After five minutes they saw a form rising in the distance, against the face of the grassy hill. The South American was climbing, still mounted on his machine, along some beaten path or sheep track.

'Full speed ahead!' Jim panted, and together they climbed in bottom gear, keeping del Pino in sight.

As midnight chimed from the moss-covered spire in Banner Village, and from the taller clocks to the west in Radford town, the curious chase went on.

16

PEPYS IN PURSUIT

PODGER HORATIO POMEROY PEPYS, Pride of
the House of Podge, Mammoth Mascot of the
Fourth and Champion Glutton of all Monks' Court,
sat up in his bed.

The door of Long Dormer had just closed. The
sound had disturbed no one: except the sleepless
Podge. He now surveyed the gloom of the long room
and pondered upon his problem. That young ass
Raymond had told him, only this evening, that the
fellows of Study Four were going on a search for
clues tonight, in 'The Case of del Pino's Bubble'.
Therefore did Sexton Pepys feel it his bounden duty
to follow those four headstrong youths.

His bed-springs uttered a muted tintinnabulation
of alarm as his prodigious form altered its disposition
and he swung a pair of legs of incredible girth to the
floor. In a moment he had snatched his gym shoes
from beneath the bed, stuffed them over his outsize
feet by the simple process of splitting half the seam,
broken the laces, muttered a suitable oath, knotted
the remaining strands with lightning vigour, and was

struggling into his trousers before you could have said 'Dr. Watson'. He began his stealthy journey to the door.

He was out of the dormer at last and closed the door with a cautious bang.

The fact that this sudden noise had awakened half the inmates of the dormitory did not trouble him, since he was unaware of the unkind comments directed from within the room at whatever person had so chosen to render the night tumultuous. Contented that he had, like the veriest wraith, slipped from his bed and had gained the corridor with no more sound than a super-criminologist should create at dead of night, he pattered down the passage upon rubber-shod feet. Nor was he in doubt of what exit had been chosen by the Quartet, since the windows alongside the West Doors were always the favourite means of egress when a fellow of the Fourth chose to exchange his comfortable bed for some private adventure in the darker hours.

There was, of course, a slight problem to be overcome. Jim Raymond and his friends measured but meanly round the waist; and even the mighty and muscular Bob Mayfield had tackled this window in his stride. But Podger Pepys was possessed of a girth more than considerable. It was therefore with much effort and many mutterings and strugglings and squeezing and leverage that he finally dropped, after the manner of a plunging water-buffalo, into the deserted Quadrangle. After which he stood up, rubbed his expansive sternsheets affectionately, and began his journey to – where?

For the first time he realized that he had not troubled to ask himself exactly where the Company of Four had gone in their search for clues in 'The Case of del Pino's Bubble'. That they had left the building was not in doubt: there had been copious signs and indications. Peering from his bed, he had noted, some fifteen minutes ago, that the fellows of Study Four had donned sweaters and slacks. They would not have done so had they been visiting some other part of the building; a dressing-gown would have sufficed upon a night as warm as this. He himself had garbed his person likewise, after their example. Not doubting that they were intending to quit the building, he had gone directly to the easiest exit, there to find, without surprise, that the window-catch by the West Doors was unfastened; and his guess was confirmed. But now that he stood in the starlit Quadrangle – where next?

Then his blade-sharp intelligence came to his aid. Surely they were not expecting to discover any clues within the grounds of the School? There were only the Head's garden, the playing-fields, the fives court, the cricket pavilion and the Gymnasium. So they must have left the grounds, as well as the building.

Sexton Pepys moved off, with no sound louder than the heavy thumping of his enormous feet to break the silence of the night. Walking directly towards the low wall that, like the windows in West Hall, was the favourite means of egress from these precincts, he halted, half-way there. For on his right, at this point, was the long, dark outline of the cycle-sheds.

Here was a new thought. Had they climbed the wall, to proceed to whatever place was their destination – on foot? Or was their journey sufficiently long to warrant bicycles? There was only one way in which to find out, and when he had, after considerable mental stress, discovered it, he moved along the front of the sheds, looking for four bicycles that were not there: and at last he came to them. They were, of course, represented by a wide space, and four empty cycle-stands.

'So . . .' muttered the keen criminologist. In a moment he had picked his own machine from the long phalanx, had wheeled it out, and was riding ponderously across the rest of the Quad towards the wall beyond which lay the road to Radford town.

Applying his brakes, which, owing to the enormous weight of this rider, were practically powerless to arrest his speed, he plunged towards the wall, observed it nearing at an uncomfortable speed, and at the last moment slewed his machine sideways and arrested his flight with one foot on the wall and the other pinned beneath a pedal.

Picking himself up and rubbing his ankle tenderly, he was not for one moment daunted. It was the work of a moment to seize his bicycle, totter with it above his head until some of its protruding components caught on the top of the wall, and climb up, dragging it over with him. It landed with a slight rasp of metal; he himself descended with a careful thud.

'Silly bounders . . .' he muttered, nonplussed.

He looked about him. The night seemed empty,

save of starlight and silence. He could not know that approximately four hundred yards distant the Quartet were waiting and watching among the bushes at the end of South Meadow.

'Headstrong young idiots . . .' he murmured, wishing, somehow, that they would show up before the night grew older. The starlight gave a strange, unearthly pallor to the countryside; the trees appeared to rear in malevolent, listening array; and the owl that was hooting mournfully above Banner Wood sent a shiver of uneasiness down the spine of Horatio Pomeroy.

'Oh, well . . .' he said, to hear the familiar and comfortable tone of his own voice, 'I'd better do something, that's what I'd better do.'

For the first time tonight Fate was beside him at last. Some guardian angel, whose high duty it was to watch over the peculiar affairs of Horatio Podge, now tossed him a morsel of good luck; and he did not ignore it.

The fact was that, just as he reached the hedgerow bordering South Meadow, Jim Raymond and Bob Mayfield, who had seen del Pino ride through the gap in the fence alongside, rode through that gap from the other direction.

Stifling a hoot of terror, Podger Pepys wobbled on his machine, righted it, wobbled again, and found himself half-buried in the ditch. It was, perhaps, the same Personal Angel belonging to Pomeroy Pepys who decreed that the ditch should, at this moment, be perfectly dry; or perhaps it was that in high summer it always was.

'Beasts!' he spluttered. 'Knocking a fellow into the ditch! Dangerous asses!'

He removed one of the pedals from his ear, prised his chin clear of the chain, clambered back to the road, dragged his machine upright, and hurled it bodily at the gap in the fence, bouncing into the sagging saddle as he did so.

Thus it came to pass, upon this night of curious events, that at the moment when Jim Raymond and Bob Mayfield were riding into the fringe of trees that bordered Banner Wood, and giving chase to del Pino ahead of them, Podger Pepys, sleuth of sleuths and king of criminologists, was bumping and shuddering over the short grass of South Meadow, fifty yards behind them.

A sixth rider had joined the chase of the Flying Bubble.

17

THE 'BUBBLE' VANISHES

THE general pattern of this midnight excursion was now becoming clear. Over the great starlit brow of Harleyfield Downs there floated the Bubble, airy and soundless in the sky.

Up the winding pathway that ran to the skyline across the chalky slopes there rode del Pino alone. Behind him, out of earshot but just within sight, came Jim Raymond and Bob, keeping pace but also keeping their distance in case the South American should look back and scan the slopes. Up the more gradual hill, a few hundred yards to the west, rode Dresley Burgess and Gregory Stevens. The other three riders were out of their sight, and they were not aware of them. All these two on the road could see was the moving shape high above their heads, and this they followed, straining at the pedals. The sixth member of this remarkable company was struggling, at this moment, to free his machine from some obstinate gorse-bushes at the bottom of the Downs. He had not glimpsed the leader, del Pino, at any period of his nightmare journey. He had not seen

Dresley or Gregory, who were following the road in the distance. He had certainly seen Jim and Bob as they had plunged into Banner Wood, but of these he had soon lost track when a large oak tree had got up and struck his hurtling bicycle, sending him spinning into the depths of a sweet-scented dell. There was, however, one thing Podger Pepys had seen, and could, if he strained his gaze, still make out against the night heavens; and that was, of course, the drifting shape of the Bubble, high above the Downs.

If the perspiring Podge had lost track of the other riders for the moment he was now aware of their destination – and that was obviously wherever the balloon was going. Even to his limited intelligence it had become clear enough that there was a chase on, and that the quarry was the balloon.

Not bothering himself with the trivial question of how he was to reach the balloon in order to grapple with it on his very unairworthy bicycle, he picked his machine bodily from the gorse bushes, tore a branch or two of prickles from his hair, and leapt again to the saddle like Buffalo Bill of old, to storm the chalky slopes with energy regained.

Well ahead of him, and a good fifty yards off his course, Jim Raymond and Bob Mayfield topped the brow of the Downs. And it was now that the strangest event of all this night's curious occurrences took place.

Jim had 'reined-in' his bicycle in order to locate del Pino by listening in silence for a moment. With Bob halted beside him, he steadied his partly-spent breath, and together they listened, scanning the sky and then the slopes below, where the Downs descended to the scattered village of Harleyfield.

Above them, faintly now, the Bubble drifted. Below them, for another moment, moved the small black form that was del Pino, riding down the lower slopes. Then, as Jim Raymond stared upwards at the Bubble it – slowly – disappeared.

In the same instant Bob Mayfield lost sight of the South American. Just now he had been moving swiftly – probably free-wheeling at a good pace – along some chalky pathway; now he was gone, as though the Downs had swallowed him.

'He's gone,' murmured Bob, peering intently but in vain.

'So has the Bubble!' said Jim, pointing upwards. They both stared; and, staring, saw nothing but the great canvas of the skies, spangled with the jewels of the starfields. A strange silence – the atmosphere of a breath suddenly held – had come to the night.

Jim frowned in puzzlement.

'Have we been dreaming, Bob?' he asked queerly.

'Of course not! The thing's just drifted out of sight, that's all! Or it's risen suddenly, and being almost transparent it's invisible now that it's higher.'

'And where's del Pino?'

'Probably come a mucker on his speed-iron – or the path has gone round a bend behind some of those bushes!'

Jim gazed skywards, then lowered his eyes to scan the Downs again. Bob's foot dropped resolutely on to a pedal.

'Come on, Jim.'

'Hold on, Bob!' Jim jerked out a hand, catching his friend's sleeve. 'Noticed anything?'

Bob peered intently again across the starlit countryside.

'No,' he shook his head. 'Give me a clue, dear boy.'

Jim pointed straight ahead to where the valley spread wide from the skirt of the Downs.

'There's the village – you can see the roofs and farms. And what's that huddle of buildings just beyond?'

Bob stared, seeing the low, dark shapes of buildings utterly unlike any of those that comprised Harleyfield Village. They were separated from it by a couple of miles of open country, an expanse of grass peppered with gorse and scrub.

'You mean the Research Station?' he asked Jim.

'Exactly. The Harleyfield Research Station. Twig yet?'

Bob shrugged, puzzled.

'Can't say I do. All I know about the place is that the Army uses it for testing tanks or something like that—'

'Whatever it's testing,' Jim cut in, 'that Flying Bubble seems to know about it. We've followed it from Monks' Court to here – about five miles; and as soon as it gets near the Research Station it vanishes!'

Bob gave a soft whistle.

'Well, shiver me giddy timbers, skipper! You think— But surely del Pino isn't playing that sort of game!'

'Who knows? Isn't that why we're here – to find out? Come on, before it's too late!'

Bob Mayfield found himself alone. Jim was slinging his bicycle at the narrow track of chalk that twisted downwards from the brow of grassy ground. Before he was swerving down between the scattered bushes of the lower slopes, straining to keep in the saddle as the wheels hit and skidded over chips of chalk and small molehills, Bob was behind him hurtling in his wake like a juggernaut upon a jet-propelled mangle, his tyres slewing and sliding over the dewy grass when he left the path and then strove to regain it. The air sang past their ears, stinging their eyes until the tears streaked back over their temples.

Within five minutes of their starting off from the brow of Harleyfield Downs they were speeding through the quiet main street of the village. A saloon car, coming from the opposite direction, blinded the two cyclists for a moment before the driver dipped his headlamps. Small stones and eddies of dust scattered around them, and the car was gone, making for the Downs. An owl, swooping low across the hedgerows, missed Bob's head by inches, and as he ducked, his control was relinquished for an instant. The next thing he knew was that his machine was streaking for a farm gate, and he leaned sharply to his left, going into a long slide that took him across the grass verge and sent him sideways into a shallow ditch, with his bicycle kicking and bucking among the sprigs of beech.

Bob's chain had been jerked off the sprocket,

but it was not broken. Wheeling his machine backwards for a few feet, he fixed the links and followed in the wake of the determined Jim Raymond.

For an hour Jim and Bob searched the roads and lanes in the vicinity of the Research Station; and once were hailed by a sentry and were obliged to jab their pedals in full flight, half expecting a bullet to come ploughing over their heads. For an hour they toured, halting many times to listen and scan the terrain for a glimpse of the Flying Bubble or of del Pino, its mysterious operator. They heard nothing but the call of night-birds, saw nothing but the stars, the clustered huts and sheds of the Station, and spasmodic traffic along the main London – Brighton road in the far distance.

'Well,' said Bob Mayfield, 'we've drawn a beautiful blank, old lad.'

Jim shrugged.

'Not entirely, Bob. The balloon's vanished; del Pino has hopped it; but at last it's given us a new clue or two. Ten to one the Bubble is something to do with the Harleyfield Research Station – and that's why del Pino has been flying it from the School over the Downs.'

They mounted their machines again and climbed the slight rise into the village. Beyond the deserted main street they turned off left, and were beginning the laborious ascent to the brow of the Downs when a dark form shot past them, followed in a moment by another.

'Dres!' shouted Jim Raymond, dismounting.

142

'Greg, you chump!' roared Bob Mayfield, stopping.

In a few minutes Gregory Stevens and Dresley Burgess came panting up the hill-road.

'Seen anything?' asked Dresley, halting his machine.

'Yes, a large owl,' nodded Bob, 'that nearly took my head off!'

'Where did you chaps get to?' asked Jim.

Gregory leaned over his handlebars, puffing.

'Dresley Burgess, Esquire,' he explained simply, 'chose to jump a hayrick with his bicycle, coming down the hill about half an hour ago. It took until now to get the hayseeds out of his chain.'

'That was after Gregory Stevens, Esquire,' added Dresley, 'had hit the side of a stray barn when coming gently round one of the more vicious corners. But we saw the Bubble vanish, anyhow.'

'Where?' asked Jim expectantly.

'Immediately above the village. It was drifting towards the Research Station, and then it seemed to rise suddenly – and that was that. All we were left with were a few million stars to look at.'

'And you know what *we* think,' added Dresley; '*we* think del Pino has got some sort of curiosity about that Research Station. That's why—'

'Save it, old bean,' said Bob Mayfield. 'We've come to the same conclusion – if it can be called a conclusion.'

'And how did del Pino manage to vanish, together with his Invisible Blimp?' asked Dresley as they left the road at the brow of the Downs and took to the short route across the grass.

'I think he must have caught our scent,' suggested Bob Mayfield. 'He got to the bushes and then hid himself until we were well past him.'

'On the other hand,' put in Jim Raymond, 'how did he—'

'*Tally-ho!*' roared Bob Mayfield, cutting him short. Jim started. 'What the—'

'Follow me, you varlets!' hooted the strident Bob, and already he was careering across the downs, back to the roadway that wound downwards towards Banner Wood. In a moment the other three were on his tail, driving their machines as hard as they could.

'Del Pino rides again!' came Bob's mighty roar. 'I did glimpse the knave upon yonder highway but a moment gone!'

'There he goes!' called Jim Raymond, as he picked out the single rider ahead of them.

Past the fork in the road, past Banner Wood, into the mile stretch to Banner village rode the four of them, now coming up close on the quarry's heels. Ahead of them by less than a dozen yards, he wobbled as he strove to keep them at a safe distance, but now Bob Mayfield, well ahead of his three comrades, made his final attack.

Shaping to pass, on a gradual bend, he uttered a last blood-curdling bellow and then swerved to his left, bearing down on the lone rider as a cruiser would bore into the exposed beam of a destroyer.

'*Help! Keep off, you b-b-beasts!*' came the final agonized hoot from the beaten quarry, and the next moment he went pitching headlong into a clump of bushes at the fringe of the grass verge, his machine somersaulting and then crashing sidewards into the nearby ditch. Bob lost his balance after his left shoulder had bumped heartily against the victim's, and his bicycle gave a lurch, a dive, and then swooped with a howl of tyres for the hedge, sending the vociferous Mayfield spinning into the thorny briars while his machine bucked once and then teetered like a skittle in the wind, to crash down within a yard of the other one in the ditch.

Jim, Dresley and Gregory swerved to avoid the general confusion and then brought their machines round with the brakes locked and the tyres screaming over the smooth road surface.

'Leave me alone, you d-dangerous d-d-devils!' came a high-pitched wail from among the bushes. Jim, Dres and Gregory looked at one another in the pale starlight; and the leather-lunged tones of Bob Mayfield lifted from the depths of the briar hedge:

'Well, shiver me yardarm with a giddy belaying-pin – it isn't del Pino at all! It's that bulldozing banshee, Peepers Podge, the Pride o' the Pork Brigade!'

18

ON THE CARPET

'Pepys!'

Silence.

'*Pepys!*'

Silence – until 'Yank' Hopkins, in the next desk, gave the rotund slumberer a warning jab in the ribs.

'*Ooch!* Go 'way!'

'Hopkins! Kindly cease endeavouring to rouse that lazy boy!'

'Yes, sir, I beg your pardon.'

Mr. Jackersby left his rostrum and walked slowly down to the fifth desk from the front of the class. The day was warm – exceptionally so – and the House-master of Winston was not feeling particularly ener-getic himself this morning. He had his work to do, however, as had his pupils, and dozing in form was not to be countenanced.

Mr. Jackersby approached the fifth desk fully prepared to rouse the corpulent Van Winkle effec-tively. The master had, on his own desk, a small jar of water that, in conjunction with a soft sponge, he used for wiping his blackboard clean. This jar was now in his hand.

The Fourth was breathless with expectancy as the thirty-odd members watched the small jar lifted in the hand of Mr. Jackersby, and as the water trickled down upon that bowed and snoring head, mirth triumphed over order, and a roar of laughter went up.

'*Ouch!* Go 'way, you silly clown! Help, I'm d-drowning! Throw me a lifeb-belt! Keep off, you lunatic!' And the plump arms of the portly Podge began flailing desperately, as they might have done had he been striking out for the distant shore from the waves of a stormy sea.

'*Pepys!*' thundered Mr. Jackersby.

'Oh, c-crumbs, it's you, sir!'

'It is assuredly I,' nodded the towering House-master, regarding his heavy-eyed pupil in a mixture of wrath and some slight bewilderment. Even this troublesome member of his class had never been known to fall fast asleep so early in the morning.

'Er . . .' bleated the hapless Pepys— 'er . . . the s-sum of two s-sides of a quadrilateral triangle are equal to half the . . . I mean I *hic, haec, hoc, hunc, hanc, hoc*—'

'Cease!' commanded Mr. Jackersby.

'Oh golly . . . !'

'Did you not go to bed last night, Pepys?'

'Oh yes, sir! B-but I couldn't s-sleep! I mean I went s-sleep-walking down to the d-dining-hall! Th-that is to say I fell in the d-ditch! I mean I lost the b-balloon and . . .'

'*Really*, my good Pepys!' cut in Mr. Jackersby as another hoot of mirth rose from the form.

'P-please can I g-go and lie down, sir?'

Mr. Jackersby stared.

'Have you a headache, Pepys?'

'Yes, sir – I mean no, sir, it's my – er – lumbago! I mean gout – that is t-to say I've sprained my ear, sir!'

The laughter that followed this statement of the corpulent victim's various ills was so loud and lasting that the Housemaster swung round.

'Silence! This is not a bear-garden!' He turned back to the unhappy Podger as the rest of the fellows did their level best to restrain their spirits. 'Pepys, you will be good enough to present yourself to Dr. Ransome immediately this class has terminated. You will take with you a note I shall give you.'

No further laughter was heard. Even the last irrepressible titter was silenced by this awful sentence. For a fellow to have to report to the Head himself, with a note stating that he had been asleep in form, was a dire matter indeed.

'B-but, sir, I – I was just closing my eyes to k-keep the sun out of . . .'

'That is enough, Pepys!'

Mr. Jackersby returned to his desk. Podger Pepys sat upright, not daring even to lean one arm upon his own. He was now shocked into full consciousness by the sentence just pronounced upon him. His rotund countenance was a portrait of abysmal woe.

'Hopkins, kindly construe!'

The American boy got to his feet, book in hand. The rest of the class composed themselves as best they might after this highly entertaining diversion. But, as 'Yank' Hopkins began his task, Jim Raymond, himself heavy-eyed and stifling a series of yawns, took his pencil and a scrap of exercise paper and scribbled a brief note. Folding it, he passed it surreptitiously to Blairman, on his left, and as Hopkins went on with his construing the note passed quietly from desk to desk, until Podger Pepys saw it slide on to the lid of his own.

With an anxious glance at Mr. Jackersby, who was, however, not looking in his direction, the miserable Podge unfolded the scrap of paper and read the few words upon it:

Don't worry: I'll get you off as soon as class is over – Raymond.

Wretched though the sleepless Pepys was feeling at this moment, he cast a faint grin of relief at Jim Raymond, and nodded, pocketing the note. The class continued, as minute by minute passed in the warm, sunlit room until, with a sound that brought a sigh of relief from almost the entire form, the bell tolled, heralding 'break'. Desks were opened, books were dumped in, lids banged, and the fellows began trooping out for a quarter of an hour in the sunny Quadrangle.

Bob Mayfield nudged his chief as he prepared to leave with the others.

'What's in the wind, skipper?'

'I'm seeing Jacko,' whispered Jim Raymond. 'I'll meet you chaps later.'

Bob, Dresley and Gregory went out with the rest. Podger Pepys was left, as a porpoise upon a low tide, standing anxiously by Mr. Jackersby's desk. The Housemaster was writing the awful terrifying note to Dr. Ransome.

Waiting until his hand had stopped writing, Jim spoke up:

'May I speak to you for a moment, sir?'

Mr. Jackersby looked up.

'Wait outside, Raymond; I wish to see Pepys first.'

'It's to do with that, sir. I'm responsible for what happened.'

'You are responsible?' Mr. Jackersby stared at the Head Boy. 'Did you drop a sleeping-draught into Pepys's cup of tea at breakfast then?'

Jim refrained from smiling.

'No, sir. But I'm afraid five of us broke bounds last night, and had no sleep.'

The Housemaster stood up wearily. The day was warm and drowsy enough, without these youngsters bringing him annoying problems.

'Let me hear all about it then. Follow me to the Quadrangle, you two boys; this building is becoming as oppressive as an oven.'

Together they went with their Housemaster into the Quadrangle, and, as soon as they had reached the cool shade of the avenue of beeches, Mr. Jackersby said:

'Well, Raymond, I am listening.'

.   .   .   .   .

It was some ten minutes after the 'break' period had ended when Mr. Jackersby came out of the Headmaster's Study. In the passage were Raymond, Burgess, Stevens, Mayfield and Pepys. Mr. Jackersby closed the door.

'Raymond, you and these other boys can cut to the Sanatorium. Matron will ensure that you sleep until lunch-time, all of you. After lunch, report to Dr. Ransome here, at two o'clock. Is that clear?'

'Yes, sir.'

'Very well; get along straight away, and tell Matron why you've been sent.'

He walked off down the corridor, his gown flowing behind him. Jim jerked his head to his friends.

'Come on, you men. Kip for little us, till lunch. How's that for a good morning programme, Podger?'

'I think we should do it every day,' grinned Pepys cheerfully. 'I say, how did you get me off seeing His Nibs?'

'I had to tell Jacko about last night, as soon as he told you to clear off when we were in the Quad.'

'So you get three of your best friends into a jam,' grunted Dresley Burgess, 'in order to save this fat bounder's neck!'

Bob Mayfield chuckled.

'Treason!' he said. 'Sheer giddy mutiny!'

Jim shrugged. 'I was going to tell Jacko about our little trip last night in any case,' he said. 'The affair's getting too serious to keep dark any longer.'

'What did Jacko tell the Old Man?' Gregory Stevens asked.

'I've no idea – I was outside the Study with you.

But it's my guess that he told him the story I gave Jacko at break.'

Bob Mayfield sighed wearily as they reached the long, cool Sanatorium. 'Which means, my faithful cuddies, that ye noble mogul is goin' to pop a pretty question or three anent ye giddy goin's-on during the nocturnal hiatus.'

'The sooner you learn some simple English, the better we shall understand you,' observed Dresley Burgess; but for the moment they were more interested in the comforting thought that in a few minutes they would be fast asleep in the peaceful San. All problems, anxieties and other distasteful considerations could, for the nonce, go ignored.

. . . . .

The Company of Four, however, were awakened in time for a salad lunch. They had passed a couple of hours in deep slumber, and were refreshed a little by a cold shower before going down to the dining-hall. But, after lunch, they were invited to pay the reckoning; and the reckoning took the form of a very searching inquiry by Dr. Ransome in person.

He listened for some ten or fifteen minutes while Jim Raymond, as spokesman, explained that he and his friends had been determined to discover the reason for the new boy's strange attitude; that they had connected del Pino's mysterious absences and activities with the Flying Bubble; and that they had, last night, set out to find the final solution to the problem.

For some time Dr. Ransome said nothing. The Quartet and Podger Pepys sat expectantly, awaiting judgement. It came.

'In the first place,' the Head began, removing his spectacles and polishing them carefully, 'you five boys will be confined to the grounds for one week. That will be your penalty for breaking bounds last night. Whatever your reason and intention in doing so, it was clear to you that you were engaged in an activity that necessitated breaking one of the fundamental rules of Monks' Court. Had you been out upon some frivolous venture I should, of course, have awarded a more serious punishment. So much for that.'

Jim Raymond pursed his lips. He was doubtful now of the wisdom of his going to Mr. Jackersby and admitting their escapade. A 'gating' was not serious, but he had landed his friends into the punishment without having first consulted them.

'For the rest of the matter,' Dr. Ransome continued, placing his spectacles on his nose and regarding each of them in turn, 'it may well be that I shall ultimately have the pleasure of congratulating you upon your acumen and your determination to clear up a very strange puzzle. You may or may not have helped considerably to forestall some plan or other before it has the necessary opportunity to reach fruition. We shall see. For the moment I shall see this boy del Pino and will endeavour to discover the truth from him.'

He glanced at Jim Raymond keenly, and added: 'It may seem to you that, in revealing what you have, you might be regarded as having 'sneaked' upon a fellow member of the School. That would be foolish to presume. The fact is, of course, that you have acted in the best interests, and might well have saved this newcomer from very serious consequences of his own folly, in curtailing his remarkable activities. You need have no conscience upon that score. I think that is all I have to say at the moment. Please remember that you are gated for one week from today, and do not let it escape your notice that in awarding this slight punishment I am also placing you all in a position in which it will be easier for me to summon you for further questioning should the necessity arise. I should not like to have to cast a net of masters and prefects over the surrounding country-side if, upon any evening during the coming week, I wished to question you suddenly.'

As the five fellows trooped out in silence, Dr. Ransome spoke once more.

'Raymond, kindly offer my compliments to Mr. Jackersby, and tell him that I have excused you five people from Preparation this evening, so that you may retire to bed an hour or so earlier.'

'I say, that's jolly g— I mean yes, sir!' replied Jim Raymond cheerfully, and closed the door.

As they made their way to the classrooms for afternoon school, Bob Mayfield shrugged.

'Gated for a week,' he said gloomily.

'Worse than a Third Form tell-tale,' nodded Dresley Burgess gravely. 'Always toadying the beaks, have you chaps noticed?'

'I must say it's a bit thick,' agreed Podger Pepys,

glad of an opportunity of exhibiting an air of pained righteousness with the backing of Mayfield, Burgess and Stevens. 'I—'

'Cease, ye bulldozing buccaneer,' cut in Bob warmly – for Pepys was not clowning, as they had been. 'If you hadn't been such an ass as to snore so loudly during Latin this would never have happened!'

'Well, really, Mayfield! At my own personal risk, I went out last night to protect you fellows from – er – from your own misguided folly, and—'

'And finished up by biffing me into a giddy bramble-tree!' nodded Bob. 'If you're not careful, my plump twinkle-toes, I'll—'

'He's perfectly right,' said Jim Raymond seriously. 'I should have asked what you chaps thought before I said anything to old Jacko.'

'You did the only possible thing, dear boy,' Dresley Burgess retorted. 'We had to tell the Old Man in any case, before that ass del Pino blew up the countryside with an atomic fire-cracker, or whatever he's aiming to do.'

'Even so . . .' shrugged Jim, 'I admit I—'

'Never mind your conscience, Jimmy,' cut in Gregory Stevens, 'because I for one don't want to leave School for a week. I've got serious work to do.'

'What sort?' asked Bob Mayfield as they reached their classroom.

'If the Old Man doesn't get anything out of del Pino, I'm going to solve the whole thing with one blow.'

They stopped, looking at him.

'How d'you mean, Greggy?'

He wrinkled his freckled nose mysteriously.

'I'll tell you the details later,' he said cryptically, 'but for the present you can call it "Operation Interception".'

And they failed to get any more from him on the subject before they joined their form for afternoon school. Had they guessed Gregory Stevens's plans they would have found it hard to concentrate upon their work, for those plans were intriguing in the very extreme.

19

THE MASTER PLAN

THE Company of Four, with permission to go to bed two hours earlier instead of doing Prep, did not, however, take advantage of their unusual privilege. Afternoon school had dragged to its warm and weary conclusion, and by tea-time the Quartet were ready for bed, but it was a few minutes after they had strolled up to Long Dormer when they got the first word of the rumour.

Podger Pepys, the other member of the Fourth who had been allowed to miss Prep, was also thinking of availing himself of this opportunity – of sleeping, comfortable and peaceful in the snug confines of the sheets, while the rest of the School was plodding miserably through Preparation. But for Podger Pepys, also, there was to be no early-to-bed this evening. It was this particular purveyor of portents and important promulgations who first had the word from young Carstairs of Four-B; and it took the chief gossip of Monks' Court no time at all to lengthen the chain of rumour that was beginning to jingle among the Studies, the J.C.R. and the Gymnasium, where several chaps were polishing up their footwork and gym-drill.

'Have you heard?' piped the irrepressible rumour-monger, regarding them with wide and excited eyes.

'We have,' grunted the weary Bob Mayfield; 'the good Queen Anne has at last passed from our midst in mortal circumstances.'

Jim Raymond chuckled.

'Come to bed, you noisy ass, before you shout the place down.'

'Really, Raymond! I came all the way up here in order to convey to you fellows a vital item of information appertaining to a matter closely concerned with—'

'Hang him upside-down!' groaned Dres Burgess, 'and shake that dictionary out.'

'Well, I *must* say, Burgess!'

'If you must, then, you must, old bean. Cough it up, and then we might have some peace.'

'That ass del Pino can't be found!'

'Can't be found?' asked Jim Raymond seriously.

'He's missing!'

'Missing?' queried Bob Mayfield, eyeing their informant.

'He's vanished!' persisted the portly Podge impressively.

'Vanished?' echoed Gregory Stevens, and sat down on his bed. 'How d'you know?'

Pomeroy swelled with importance. Horatio was inflated with information. Pepys palpitated to dispense the knowledge so recently garnered from young Carstairs.

'My dear fellow, I just *know*! Everyone knows — I mean they know now I've told them! I was the first to hear, of course. I may have my faults, but no one can say I don't keep a sharp eye out for interesting news. We criminologists, you know, must always be on the alert for scraps of infor—'

'Turn him off, somebody, turn him off at the main!'

'Get to the point, Podger,' nodded Jim Raymond.

'Very well, I shall – if you fellows will kindly cease to interrupt. Del Pino's missing, that's the whole point of the matter. The Old Man sent for him soon after we left his Study – and he couldn't be found. You remember when Dakers came in and spoke quietly to Old Harry during Geology this afternoon? Well, he was asking if the old boy had seen the missing del Pino! Everyone's been looking for him all the afternoon!'

Jim Raymond sat on his bed, swinging a shoe, but he made no further effort to undress and climb in. This news was important. To give Podger his due, he had brought information that was much more than idle gossip. The Quartet, with Pepys's doubtful assistance, was still eager to solve. 'The Case of del Pino's Bubble', and this news might help considerably. It seemed, in view of it, that the new boy had decided to run to earth. The end of the puzzle might be in sight, once he was discovered.

'Who's for bed now?' asked the leader of the Company of Four, looking round at his friends.

'Not me,' said Bob readily.

'Not I,' corrected Dresley Burgess.

'But what can we do about it?' asked Gregory Stevens.

Jim looked at him.

'We can find him, for a start, old bean.'

Gregory shook his head.

'You chaps can go and see if you can get on to his scent, by making the usual sort of search. Frankly, I think I shall find where he is much more quickly – and by a rather amusing method.' And he began undressing, saying no more.

'By going to bed?' said Bob in bewilderment.

'No, I'm going to take a good cold shower, then I'm off.'

'Where to?'

'Not in front of the children . . .' was his cryptic reply.

Podger Pepys pouted, taking 'the children' to mean himself.

'Well, I *must* say, Stevens! As the prime investigator in this baffling case, I—'

'Listen, twinkletoes,' said Gregory gravely, 'you joined in our little expedition last night, and what happened? You clouted Bob into a bramble-forest, buckled your bike in the process, and then got us all into a jam this morning through falling asleep in form!'

'In all fairness to our dear Podge,' cut in Bob Mayfield with a grin, 'you've got things t'other way round – it was I who sent him into the ditch, with malice aforethought and a lunge with my left shoulder.'

'Thank you, Mayfield,' acknowledged Pepys righteously.

'Not at all, old chap. Do the same for you again, whenever you say the word.'

'Anyway,' chuckled Jim Raymond, 'I'm going down to the Study for a book. If I go to bed I shan't sleep without a chapter or two to tire me out.' Saying which, he left the dormer, followed by Dres Burgess, who was taking the hint.

Gregory Stevens made his exit, to take a cold shower in the bathrooms. Podger Pepys blinked, seeing the retreating form of Bob Mayfield, who was following Jim and Dresley down the corridor. But although the audience was filing out, the energetic Podger could raise his little curtain once again, by seeking others of Winston House whom the news of del Pino had yet to reach.

In a moment he was bowling boisterously down to the Junior Common Room, intent upon new ears for his exciting story.

In the privacy of Study Four, Jim Raymond turned to Bob and Dresley.

'I don't know what old Gregory has got up his sleeve,' he said quietly, 'but I think we should stand by to help him do whatever he's got in mind. What say you, chaps?'

'He said he was going to find del Pino,' shrugged the muscular Bob. 'That's a fair enough game for me. More excitin' than bye-byes, anyway.'

'I'm in,' nodded Dresley. They settled down to wait for the fourth member of their Company, and in ten minutes he was down from the shower, looking spruced and refreshed.

'What's the angle, Greg?' Jim asked straight away.

Gregory closed the door quietly.

'The angle, my angels, is simply that I think del Pino is hiding up because if once the Head gets on to him he's finished – and so are his merry little plans.'

Jim watched him intently.

'You mean he's still aiming to fly that Bubble again tonight?'

'I think so. If the Old Man puts the pressure on him, he'll either have to give his little game away, or he'll have to lie his way out, or, thirdly, he might just remain stubbornly silent. In any of those three cases, unless he's a superlative fibber, the Head's going to shove him in the San under Matron's charge – and there'll be no more Bubble-flying for him.'

Dresley nodded slowly.

'So you think that's why he's scooted?'

'I do. It's only a guess. If he hadn't shown up in School since last night's ride over the Downs, I'd say something had happened to him – an accident on his bike, or something serious. As things are, we saw him in School this morning, just as though he hadn't been out of the dormer last night.'

'I suppose it *was* del Pino we followed through Banner Wood last night?' put in Bob Mayfield.

'I'd bet on it,' nodded Jim. 'Everything points to him.'

'Well,' shrugged Bob, 'we thought it was del Pino when we followed him back, along the road – but it was Horatio Podge I biffed into the ditch.'

'It wasn't Podge who was riding ahead of us through the Wood, though,' pointed out Jim Raymond. 'We got his story from him, and every word of it allowed for del Pino's being abroad on the Downs.'

Gregory leaned on the windowsill, looking out to where the sun was setting above the playing-fields, firing the hill-rims above Radford town.

'Anyway, I'm going after friend del Pino tonight,' he said confidently, 'and we shall see a lot of things more clearly when I've found him.'

Jim Raymond glanced at him. He knew Gregory Stevens for a serious, intelligent chap, whose schemes – other than those connected with his terrifying super-kite – were never hare-brained or haphazard. He thought, for reasons known to himself alone, that he could find del Pino, unaided by authority. Jim Raymond would have backed him up willingly, knowing as he did that when old Greg set himself a task it was usually completed with success.

'All right, Greg,' he said evenly, 'tell us the details. If you want us to help, that's to say.'

'You can come along, by all means, Jim – so can Bob and Dresley; but I don't fancy I shall need any help, exactly. It's a one-man job, but if you want to watch, it might turn out to be amusing.'

Casual as his tone was, careless as were the words, they were intrigued, rather than deterred. Greggy was out for some fun, and they wanted to be there.

'Count me in,' said Dresley, and Bob nodded vigorously.

Jim said: 'I'm game. But we shall have to know something about it, shan't we?'

'Not necessary,' murmured Gregory, perhaps enjoying the mystification he was causing. 'But for your information, my plans are pretty simple. They're these: if the wind's in the same quarter as it was last night, I think del Pino is going to float his Bubble. If he does, then I'm going to bring it down. That's all. Call it "Operation Interception", as I said this afternoon. By the way, there's a way in which you *can* help, come to think of it.'

They were silent, trying to guess his intentions. The cryptic phrase – 'Operation Interception' – meant nothing at all to them, without knowing more about the details.

'Well?' asked Jim at last.

'You've a pair of field-glasses, Jimmy, haven't you?'

'I have.'

'Good. Can you bring 'em along?'

'Of course.'

'Fine. That's all we shall need.' He lowered himself casually from his perch on the windowsill. 'Now I'm going to toddle off down to the Quad. Wind-testing, you know. If it's changed, the Bubble won't fly, and the programme's off. But somehow I don't think it has. It was coming nor'-west not long after tea-time, and it's probably set for the night. Shan't be long.'

The door closed on him.

Jim looked at his friends.

'Something tells me,' he grinned faintly, 'that tonight is going to prove interesting.'

20

MEETING IN MID-AIR

ELEVEN chimes drifted from the great clock above the central tower of Monks' Court School. The slow wind, that was moving drowsily from the Surrey hills, carried the mellow sound of these eleven chimes southwards across the trees of Banner Wood, and on beyond to Harleyfield Downs.

Few lamps burned in the ancient ramifications of the building. Here, a master sat reading, prior to bed; there, a prefect continued his studies later than he had intended; and from their windows was shed the light they worked by. But these windows were few; most of the place was in total darkness. In the Headmaster's Study, Dr. Ransome was talking with Mr. Jackersby, discussing the mystery of del Pino, the new boy from South America who had disappeared this afternoon, just at a time when he was wanted for questioning.

But these two gentlemen, concerned as they were with the serious question of the vanishing pupil, were no nearer its solution. In the morning, Dr. Ransome intended calling in the assistance of the police, and a full-scale search would be instituted; but for the moment there was this period of waiting. The boy might return before the morning. It was to be hoped for, until then.

A search had already been made of the turrets, attics and store-rooms of Monks' Court, after Jim Raymond's story had been given to the Head. But there was no turret, no garret, no corner or crevice of the ancient building that had revealed even a hint of del Pino's presence. He was, it seemed, out of bounds, possibly distantly so.

In Long Dormer, at this moment when Dr. Ransome talked with Mr. Jackersby, there were six beds vacant. One, of course, was del Pino's. Another was Jim Raymond's; a third Bob Mayfield's; a fourth Dresley Burgess's; a fifth Gregory Stevens's. The sixth was that nocturnal couch belonging to none other than His Ponderous Rotundity, Podger Pepys, Prince of Porpoises.

Where the latter was, no one knew. Not in the dormer; not out with the Company of Four. For the moment the whereabouts of the plump sleuth shall remain as a query-mark.

The Company of Four, however, were some little way from Long Dormer, and quite a distance from Monks' Court itself. Though on the trail of the missing South American, they were, curiously enough, motionless under the stars. Their hunting had assumed the form of waiting, and watching, and standing by. For the moment they, too, shall remain unseen, as the great clock sends out the chimes of eleven on this night of curious events.

Del Pino had been seen by none. Since two o'clock, when he had been observed in the vicinity of Study Six, just prior to the beginning of afternoon school, he had disappeared with such suddenness that it was not until Dr. Ransome had sent for him that he had been missed.

But, though unseen by any, del Pino was one of the principal characters of the night's curious events, and at this moment he was, unknowingly, about to play his part.

So much for the actors in the mysterious little drama that was, a few minutes after eleven o'clock, to take place. The scene was the stretch of country-side surrounding Monks' Court, and particularly that portion of it to the south of the School. The Quadrangle was deserted and lit only by the star-fields a myriad miles above. The road from Banner village to Radford town was empty of traffic; its gentle curves winding among the meadows and hedgerows, the roadway smooth and gleaming faintly in the pale starlight. South Meadow slept, though dew was rising among the grass-stems, spangling its expanse with minute reflections of the night-sky. Banner Wood lay like a great dark cushion of leaves upon the sweeping backcloth of the fields and farm-land all about.

For a few minutes after the lazy drifting of the chimes had moved to silence there came no further sound among the clustered timbers. No sound save when a fox crept, marauding; or a stoat moved, questing for food; or a badger woke from his daylight seclusion to venture abroad for his meal. There came no sound, for these few minutes, until—suddenly yet gradually—a whirring, soft but persistent, crept into the leafy silence. A whirring—a humming—a murmur—such words might describe the sound, yet there was in its voice a tone that no bird, no owl, no nocturnal insect could produce. A moment, and a moment more this sound continued, and then, as though it were the soft prelude to a spectacle, the spectacle appeared, from the depths of the shadowed trees.

There rose, gently, from the crown of leaves, the strange, transparent sphere whose name among the members of the School was now well known: the Flying Bubble. It lifted, light as a bubble from a child's clay pipe, from the leafy roof of Banner Wood; and then, as the southward-drifting breeze took it, it floated, still rising, across the meadows.

The wind was from the north, as Gregory Stevens had expected; and the Bubble was flying again tonight, as he had thought it might. It flew, slow as a thistledown upon a lazy stream, and now reached the ceiling of its gradual climb. Some two or three hundred feet, and seemingly among the very stars themselves, it drifted, southwards to the Downs.

The faint whirring of its small and curious machinery had long since faded to silence, and Jim Raymond, crouched in a knoll of saplings half-way between the wood and the Downs, did not catch its sound. With his field-glass raised, however, he saw the Bubble, and his voice came breathlessly.

'Greg! You were right—look!'

Gregory took the glasses from him, and raised

them. For a moment he gazed, then lowered them, nodding.

'Good! Coming this way at about four miles an hour; about two hundred feet up; making almost due south!' He turned to Dresley Burgess. 'Fix the hook, Dres – quickly!'

Burgess nodded, and, as Bob Mayfield held the Stevens Super-Kite upright, keeping its tail clear of the ground, he fitted the long metal hook to the top of the kite, sliding the prongs that Gregory had made into the two channels of the struts.

'Ready!' he said.

Gregory took the winder, set the ratchet to the 'off' position, and nodded to Bob Mayfield.

'Rise and shine . . .' he said briefly.

Bob moved a yard or two away, holding the kite vertical, then, at a final nod from its inventor, he lifted it, releasing the handgrips. With a quick twist of the elevator levers, Gregory pulled back on the winder, and the kite rose into the air as smoothly as an immense leaf would be whirled from a bough in a winter wind.

Bob stood back, ducking once as the great kite dipped for a moment above his head; then it lifted to a dozen feet, then fifteen, and twenty, while Gregory let the winder run, clicking over the tiny ratchet. Jim Raymond took the field-glasses again and raised them, gazing north.

'Give me a guide, Jimmy,' murmured the kite-operator, 'as soon as she nears the Bubble.'

Gregory paid out the twine as he spoke; and Jim nodded without speaking. Bob and Dresley peered upwards, watching the balloon as it came drifting, high above their heads, towards the Downs in the other direction. The plan conceived by the technical brain of the 'crank' of the Fourth was now in operation.

'Coming up,' said Jim, refocusing his glasses constantly as the balloon neared, minute after minute. 'Can you go higher, Greg?'

By way of reply, Stevens released the tension-device on the winder, and the three strings ran out with a quick whirr of acceleration from the ratchet. Slowly the kite lifted, its size, great though it was, diminishing against the canopy of the heavens.

Zero hour was near now. Gregory Stevens was staking all on the last moment of his careful plans. If he could bring down the mysterious Bubble, they could at least discover what it contained, and what was its use. At the same time they could scotch del Pino's game completely – unless he possessed another balloon, which was very doubtful. Further, they suspected that the South American would be in Banner Wood tonight, ready with his bicycle to follow the Bubble, as he had done last night. If he saw his balloon come down, he would ride up to see what had happened and, as Gregory had said so confidently, del Pino would be found more easily than by searching the countryside.

His Bubble had become, in this sense, a bait to catch its own operator. It all depended upon the last moment when Gregory had manœuvred the kite against the balloon. Above the kite there was now fixed the long, twin-pronged wire; with it they would try to hook the base of the balloon, catching at any protrusions or bracings – with luck, and with much skill.

It had been Stevens's original intention to stand by with the kite in the Quadrangle and bring down the other flyer before it had risen far from the turret, but since he had heard that every turret and attic in Monks' Court had been subjected to a rigorous search he had guessed that del Pino would be farther afield, and the most likely spot would be the concealing mass of trees, Banner Wood. He could not send up his balloon from anywhere on the Downs, as the ground was too exposed, and it might be seen from the village below. Only when it was a couple of hundred feet or more in the air was it almost invisible: therefore it had to rise from somewhere secluded. Banner Wood had been Gregory's guess, and the guess had been proved correct.

'Left a little,' called Jim, gazing with his field-glasses raised and trained on the strange, drifting sphere. 'Keep that height, it's about level, or slightly below. Left . . .'

Gregory moved a lever, slightly. Bob and Dresley watched, holding their breath. The two shapes were nearing now rapidly. Through the powerful lenses Jim saw them more clearly than did his friends. The Bubble was gliding smoothly through the air; and so transparent was the spherical 'skin' that stars winked through it from above, as through a thin cloud-haze. Beneath it there was suspended what appeared to be a small black box, and this was attached, as Jim could at last make out, by thin bracing-wires.

'Steady as you are, Greg. . . . There are bracing-wires at the base of the balloon. We should hook it nicely with any luck! Steady . . .'

The balloon floated on, now almost overhead. The darker shape of the kite hovered, as though awaiting it upon some invisible, airy pathway.

'Twenty feet apart,' cautioned Jim Raymond. 'Come down a couple of feet!'

The winder jerked; the strings trembled.

'Fifteen feet – left, left a little . . .'

One string quivered as the lever moved; the kite pulled over, with an amazing obedience of the controls.

'Steady now. . . . Ten feet . . . height perfect – you're right in its path – steady as you are. . . . Five feet . . .'

Bob Mayfield gulped. Dresley Burgess had forgotten to breathe. High above their heads the two forms drew together, making their strange, inanimate rendezvous among the stars.

'Ready, Greg! Four feet . . . three . . . two . . .'

Gregory held the winder rock-steady, waiting for the last signal. It came, sharply:

'Strike! *Strike up!*'

He jerked the main lever. Through the glasses, Jim saw the kite shudder, lifting and then clawing down with its twin-pronged hook. It missed, by inches.

'Move off . . .' said Jim, and, according to plan, Gregory began walking, at what he judged to be the speed of the floating Bubble, due southwards over the grass.

'Ready . . .' he heard Jim, 'ready . . . Now – *strike!*'

As Dresley, Bob and Gregory moved off, Jim stood motionless, his glasses trained unwaveringly. The kite shuddered again, and the hook clawed – clawed and caught, caught and – came away, with a bracing-wire of the Bubble torn from the base.

The balloon rocked, drunkenly, but its gas carried it on, drifting with the breeze, now at a lopsided angle.

'Ready!' called Jim. 'You're directly beneath!'

Gregory waited, his controls trembling to the wind across the strings. Jim's call came swiftly:

'Strike! *Strike up!*'

Through the lenses, that wide hook lifted again, and again clawed down; and this time . . .

'Keep steady, Greg – you've got it! Don't worry it!' And Jim came running over the grass towards his friends. Stopping sharply, he raised the glasses again.

'The hook's well over two of the wires – don't lift an inch or you'll lose it!'

'I'm going to wind-in,' replied Gregory. The winder moved in his hands, drawing in the three strings. He could feel, now, a slight vibration, other than that of the wind in the strings; and he guessed there was some kind of motor on board the queer Bubble, whose slight revolutions were passing down the kite-strings from the hook.

'Down . . .' Jim told him; 'slowly down . . .'

Gregory wound-in, slowly. Slowly the balloon

grew larger. First there came the dark shape of the kite, trembling a little to the tension of the strings; then the Bubble, hooked securely by the base. The strain on the strings was considerable, as the lighter-than-air gas of the balloon strove to overcome the downward pull of the kite. But it was the kite that won.

As the Flying Bubble, now nearer than anyone except del Pino had ever seen it, came down from the stars, Bob Mayfield released his breath.

'Good old Greggy! The man's a giddy genius!'

'Grand show!' cried Dres Burgess, slapping the kite-fiend on the back in his exuberance.

'Clear off, you chump – you'll ruin the works!'

But the Bubble was now only a dozen feet above their heads. Already Jim Raymond was preparing to hang on to it when it was low enough for his reach. And, a moment later, as his hands touched the bracing-wires, Bob Mayfield let out a yell:

'Look! There's the enemy! *Come on!*'

He leapt for the nearest of the four bicycles that had brought them here, and clambered astride it just as Dresley saw the dim figure of the rider who had left the road at the edge of the field to head this way, and who was now swerving on his bicycle and driving it back the way he had come.

'Del Pino!' hooted Bob, as Jim and Gregory hauled in the Bubble. 'Come back, ye skinny skulduggerer!'

Dresley was on another cycle and in pursuit of the plunging Bob within a few seconds of the outcry.

Together they shuddered over the rough grass in chase of the South American.

The Flying Bubble was captured at last; and its mysterious operator was on the run, with two of the Quartet drawing up on him minute by minute and yard by yard down the winding, starlit road.

21

HAIL HORATIO!

'Sit down, del Pino.'

The South American obeyed. Sitting in the carved-oak chair, he faced Dr. Ransome squarely, not glancing for a moment at the other members of Winston House who had been summoned to this awesome Study together with him. His left arm was still in a sling and one eye was turning black, but for all his woeful appearance he was composed enough.

He realized that this was his trial. With his Headmaster for the supreme judge and jury combined, he had the fellows of Study Four as his prosecuting witnesses. Pepys, who was also here, was yet another enemy in this 'courtroom', for the fat idiot had unearthed dangerous evidence last night, when Raymond and his friends had brought the Bubble to the ground.

Dr. Ransome seated himself at his great desk and folded his hands, perhaps deliberating upon what he had to say. Then:

'I do not intend to waste time, del Pino, in dragging your story from you, word by word. I hope you are going to co-operate, by volunteering all the information we require from you.'

The new boy said nothing, though his very silence implied antagonism.

'My first question,' went on the Head, 'is simply this: you admit to operating this curious balloon that was brought down last night?'

For a moment it seemed as if the South American were going to keep silent, whatever question was asked him. Then he appeared to give in, and spoke briefly.

'Yes, sir.'

'Good. And now tell us, please, how the device came into your possession. Did you construct it yourself?'

'No, sir.'

'Well, then?'

'I – found it.'

'Where did you find it?'

Again there was silence, and now it was so prolonged that a sudden sharpness was evident in Dr. Ransome's tone:

'Answer me, boy!'

Del Pino stiffened, as though surprised that the rather kindly attitude of his Headmaster could change so swiftly.

'I – found it at home, sir.'

'In South America, you mean?'

'Yes, sir.'

'Tell me about it, del Pino, briefly but truthfully, if you please.'

Jim Raymond and his three Study-mates listened

intently, as eager to hear the story of the Flying Bubble as was their Headmaster. It was brief enough.

'The balloon was built by enemy agents, sir, during a civil conflict in territory under my father's command.'

'Why did you bring it with you?'

'Because – well, sir, because I thought I might fly it.'

'With what purpose?'

Del Pino's answer was made in a tone slightly defensive.

'I heard talk of war, with Britain as a participant.'

Dr. Ransome's eyes jerked up to study the boy's face. Jim Raymond and his friends exchanged glances.

'War, my dear boy?' For a moment the Head seemed at a loss; then, as though remembering that the whole world had discussed the subject of war for years after the 1939–1945 struggle, he smiled faintly.

'I sincerely trust you were flagrantly misinformed,' he said gently, and dismissed this rumour for what it was worth – the overhearing of some conversation conducted by the boy's elders, themselves perhaps loosely speaking. 'So you brought your toy balloon to Britain, to help in the war. And, upon arriving here, you doubtless discovered that Monks' Court is not far from a Research Station. Is that correct?'

'Yes, sir.' Del Pino bit his lip. The reference to his balloon as a 'toy' had found its mark. Like his Bubble, he was deflated.

'And you imagined,' went on Dr. Ransome evenly,

'that the Research Station was conducting some form of secret experimental work? Such as building a death-ray machine – or perhaps designing a large bomb with which to sink the continent of South America overnight?'

'I – I heard there were experiments going on there, something to do with the atom bomb, sir.'

Dr. Ransome smiled again. There was obviously only one way in which to counter this foolish boy's romantic notions: by showing them to be childish. Otherwise they might become dangerous, when the boy was old enough to be roused to further exploits by political fever.

'Since the atom bomb was first used,' the Head continued, 'it has never left our minds – and that is a good thing, for the problem it presents to the civilized world is grave indeed. However, there *are* other matters for our deliberation, I can assure you. One of them is the subject of television – which happens to be the very interest of those scientists working at the Harleyfield Research Station.'

He looked hard at the boy for a moment, and then drove his point home:

'In fact, you must come along with me one evening, my dear del Pino, and look over the place. I can easily arrange it, as a subject of education; and you'd be most interested, I'm sure.'

The South American said nothing, but his ears burned as he returned the steady and slightly amused gaze of Dr. Ransome. This gaze now shifted, and fixed upon the device that stood at one end of the desk. Two feet high and as broad, the Flying Bubble appeared more innocent than when it had been inflated and sent among the starfields on its mysterious journeys.

'I see that your toy balloon has some kind of camera suspended from it, del Pino. Do I take it that in some way you were trying to take photographs of the Research Station from the air?'

'I – I was, sir, yes.'

'M'm. . . . Well, now that I have invited you to look over that Station, whenever we choose to make an appointment with my good friend the Chief Technician there, you can appreciate that you were going the wrong way about things – m'm?'

A sudden chuckle came from Bob Mayfield; and Dr. Ransome glanced at the Quartet, nodding gently. The idea of del Pino's elaborate plans to photograph the Harleyfield Station, when he was at liberty to inspect them educationally, was too rich for their sense of humour to be contained.

'Well now,' the Head continued, 'we should be interested in a little education ourselves, del Pino.' His hand poked a component of the Bubble. 'What is this thing, for instance?'

'An electric motor, sir.' The boy got up and came slowly to the desk, looking down at his 'toy'.

'What is it for? The gas takes the thing up, I presume, and the wind carries it along – why do you want a motor?'

'For remote control, sir. There's another on the carrier of my bicycle, and—'

'Ah, I understand, yes. Twin remote control motors, m'm? If the one on your bicycle points west, then the one on the balloon turns to point in the same direction, is that correct?'

'Yes, sir.'

'Of course. They had some at Gamages, if I remember. Very useful for model aircraft and the like. And how did you inflate this absurd contraption?'

'With a gas-cylinder, sir.'

'Ah. And where is that?'

'I – I concealed it under a floorboard, in one of the turrets.'

'Indeed.' Dr. Ransome sat back, clasping his hands on his lap and staring reflectively at the balloon. 'So you sent this ridiculous toy into the air by night when the wind was from the north, and let it drift over the Downs to the Research Station?'

'That's right, sir.'

'Following it on your bicycle. Why?'

'So that I could steer the balloon directly over the buildings, using the remote control.'

'I see. Then the camera came into action. How did you prevent the flash from illuminating the whole countryside?'

'It's an infra-red camera, sir.'

'Ah, quite. Really, del Pino, what an extraordinarily elaborate method of seeing something that can be seen merely by asking politely!'

The South American was silent. In the last few moments all the drama, all the romance and the intrigue had been stripped from his secret activities, and he stood here, a boy with a toy balloon. . . .

'Well, my dear del Pino, do you agree? That your methods were highly extraordinary?'

'I – I suppose they were, sir.'

'Of course. Of course they were. I have discovered this kind of nonsense often enough among the Third Forms, but I must admit that such an affair has never, until now, come to light among the older members of the School.' The Head gave a shrug of dismissal. 'However, I trust the affair is an isolated instance of one boy's capacity for the dramatic.' He glanced at Jim Raymond. 'You said you had some other information for me, Raymond. Let us hear it now, and finish with the matter.'

Jim stood up. 'It's really Pepys, sir, who should tell you about it. It was a discovery he made in Study Six last night.'

'B-but I n-never had anything to do with—' began Podge nervously, until Jim kicked his fat ankle by hooking a foot behind him. *'Ooooch!'* . . .' For the lawless Horatio, ever at variance with authority, could not quite appreciate that he was here, in the most dreaded Study in the whole building, to assist his Headmaster, and not to incur his wrath.

'It was a book, sir,' began Jim Raymond – but now Pepys was awake to the matter in hand.

'Oh, you m-mean the b-book, sir!' And his hand fumbled about his capacious jacket to produce the exercise-book he had lost on the playing-field. In a moment it lay open, on Dr. Ransome's desk. Jim Raymond thought it best to explain, before the confused Pomeroy could cloud the issue.

'Pepys found a note-book, sir, in his Study, in

which there was code-writing. He lost track of it, but managed to copy a line or two in his own book – the one before you, sir. It was taken by del Pino – he admitted that this morning when I asked him about it – but Pepys found it again last night.'

Dr. Ransome nodded slowly, gazing at the coded words:

Ibsmfzgjfme Sftfbsdi Tubujpo fohbhfe po bupnjd fyqfsjnfout. Xjmm buufnqu qipuphsbqit cz ojhiu vtjoh

'Will someone kindly construe?' he murmured drily.

Jim Raymond obeyed. 'It reads,' he said: '*Harley-field Research Station engaged on atomic experiments. Will attempt photographs by night, using* . . . and that was as far as Pepys was able to copy, sir.'

'Well, that will be more than sufficient. More elaboration, del Pino, m'm? I do declare that if your talents and energy were directed into sensible channels you would prove a very intelligent fellow. Tell me, did you actually take photographs?'

'Yes, sir.'

'Can you produce them?'

Saying nothing, the new boy laid three negatives upon the Headmaster's desk. Placing them over a white sheet of blotting-paper, Dr. Ransome studied them in silence for some minutes. When he spoke again there was a hint of humour in his voice.

'Well, well! If I did not know the subject of these pictures, I should have guessed that they depicted a storm at sea, a section of a cauliflower, or an area of pond-weed.'

Bob Mayfield let out a hoot of delight, that was cut short by a remindful jab in his ribs from Dresley Burgess.

'Sorry, sir,' murmured the quivering Mayfield.

'I am glad you find humour in the situation, Mayfield. I also feel moved to merriment, though not to an extent quite so vociferous.' His hands held the three negatives, and slowly ripped them across. 'Raymond, you will kindly take away this plaything here, and ask Mr. Robin to consign it to an incinerator. When it is done, report to me again.'

'Yes, sir.' As Jim lifted the Flying Bubble from the desk the Head looked steadily at del Pino.

'Remain here, del Pino. You others may go, with Raymond.'

A moment later the Company of Four found themselves in the corridor, with Podger Pepys.

'Well,' said Jim cheerfully, as he carried the Bubble before him, 'you wrapped up that little case neatly, Podger, I must say!'

'My dear Raymond,' protested the modest Pomeroy, as they made their way to Mr. Robin's boiler-house near the Quadrangle, 'without the good work and willing obedience of my four young assistants "The Case of del Pino's Bubble" might have taken quite a few days longer to elucidate.'

.   .   .   .   .

It was half an hour later when Jim returned to

Study Four, after reporting to the Head that the Flying Bubble had been well and royally consumed to cinders.

'What news from the King?' sang out Bob Mayfield as his chief entered the Study.

'In the first place,' said Jim cheerfully, 'del Pino has been given a long lecture on the subject of misdirected energy. I don't think we'll see any more bubbles floating about. In the second place, we are no longer gated.'

'I should jolly well think not!' said Gregory Stevens warmly, 'after we've risked our giddy necks solving the Great Aerial Mystery for the Old Man!'

'That's not all, old bean,' chuckled Jim. 'We four have got the day off tomorrow!'

'The – day *off*?' gasped Bob Mayfield.

'Precisely. The idea is that we should catch up on our lost beauty sleep, but the Head gave me the hint. He said we weren't necessarily under Matron's orders if we felt like a walk – and remember we're no longer gated.'

Dres Burgess nodded happily.

'I must say I've always considered the Old Man to be rather a decent type,' he conceded.

'How about Pepys?' asked Gregory.

'The same goes for him.'

'Good old Podge!' Bob Mayfield got up from his chair and paced the Study with enthusiasm. 'Tell you what we'll do tomorrow, you men! We'll take Podger to Harleyfield Downs, with a whackin' great picnic hamper – and when he gets full enough we'll watch him float upwards like the Flying Bubble!'

'That's quite an idea,' said Jim seriously. 'How much tuck can we rake together?'

Gregory Stevens poked his head into the cupboard and sang out:

'Three pork pies, two apple tarts, half a dozen cream buns and the cherry out of a long-deceased cake.'

Jim made for the door.

'All right – we'll buy some more to add to that, first thing in the morning! Now let's break the tidings to our resident criminologist!'

Within a moment there began a thunderous knocking on the door of Study Six.

'*Hoops!*' came a faint voice from within. 'Keep off, you scoundrel!'

Bob chuckled. 'He thinks it's del Pino after his fat blood for that code-book business.'

As the Quartet walked into the Study they found the corpulent crime-expert endeavouring to clamber from the window, which overlooked the roof of the fives court.

'K-keep off, you beasts! I'm n-not here! I died of lumbago, two days ag-go!'

As Jim Raymond seized the ample stern-sheets of the struggling Podge, Bob Mayfield lifted his voice anew:

'Podger Horatio Pomeroy Pepys, Last Remaining Super-Sleuth of Winston House and Prime Purloiner of all Personal Property Pertaining to Provender, ye are hereby sentenced to one day's Holiday tomorrow, according to ye great mercy of King Ransome ye First of Monks' Court!'

'You're nutty!' gasped the amazed victim of Bob's little joke.

'Furthermore,' went on the ringing tones of the sentence, 'ye are hereby commanded to repair to Harleyfield Downs by noon tomorrow, together with these gallant gentlemen, namely, Ye Honourable and Disreputable Company of Four, in order to assist them in the carrying of two large hampers of delectable tuck—'

'One of which,' grinned Dresley Burgess, 'must be consumed by yourself, without any assistance from the aforesaid scoundrels!'

'H-hampers?' gasped Pepys. 'T-tuck?' he stuttered incredulously.

'You heard your dreadful sentence aright,' intoned Bob Mayfield. 'A free tuck-in for Friar Tuck!'

'As much as he can tuck away!' grinned Gregory Stevens, and with a concerted heave they lifted the portly prisoner from the floor, to carry him from the Study and along the corridor.

'Make way!' hooted Mayfield's mighty tones, as door after door was flung open and fellows' heads appeared. 'Make way, I say! We come with Pepys, Pride of ye House of Podge!'

'P-put me down, you s-silly bounders!'

'Good old Peepers!'

'L-let me go!'

'Three cheers for Pomeroy!'

'Hurray for Horatio! Hip . . .'

'Hip-pip . . .'

'Horatio-o-o!'

Thus, and in triumph, was the famous criminologist of Monks' Court borne in all his glory down the Fourth Form corridor, a high example to all who witnessed his march of victory over the forces of evil and darkness, against whose skulduggering he had pitted his brilliant wits. Or so he saw himself, as he was carried aloft among the applauding throng. For once the portly Podge was achieving instant popularity; and he enjoyed every moment of his hour.